Italian Fairy Tales
by
Lilia E. Romano

"OH, HOW BEAUTIFUL OUR MISTRESS IS."
From "The Quest of the Bird with the Golden Tail."

Italian Fairy Tales

by
Lilia E. Romano

Illustrated by
Howard Davie

HIPPOCRENE BOOKS, INC.
New York

ISBN 0-7818-0702-6

For information, address:
HIPPOCRENE BOOKS, INC.
171 Madison Avenue
New York, NY 10016

Printed in the United States of America.

FROM "THE CHILD OF
THE MYRTLE TREE."

CONTENTS

THE WONDERS OF ITALY

ORIGINALITY is the keynote of these wonderful stories, while they are as beautiful as the beautiful country they come from.

They partake of their varied surroundings; the wildness of the snow-capped Alps; the splendour of the great forests and the mighty rushing rivers; the colours of the glorious sky, mirrored in the waters of the broad lakes; the perfume of the orange groves and myrtle trees; the luscious fruits; and the loveliness of the miles on miles of almond blossoms in the spring and the rich vineyards in the autumn-time.

The people of Italy have been renowned in Art for centuries, in Literature, Music, Painting, and Sculpture, and famous as warriors from the days of the ancient Romans.

And their fairies, I may tell you, their magicians, goblins, gnomes, and giants, are not to be outdone by the mortals. I think when you have read these grand stories you will agree that you have never heard of more charming and kindly fairies, of more terrible giants, of more wicked old witches, and of more wonderful things that are here related.

This is indeed a Wonder Book.

EDRIC VREDENBURG.

FROM "THE LEGEND OF THE WHITE CHAMOIS."

THE QUEST OF THE BIRD WITH THE GOLDEN TAIL

THERE was once upon a time, in the kingdom of San Fiaschetto, a Queen who was as proud and disagreeable as she was beautiful. One day, as she was driving about her kingdom, she saw at the door of a poor cottage a little lame and humpbacked boy. The wicked Queen, who hated the sight of ugly things, began laughing scornfully, so that the boy began to weep; and the boy's mother, who was inside the cottage, feeling very miserable and vexed, went to the fairies, complaining of the bad Queen who had laughed at a poor cripple.

" The Queen shall know all about this," said the fairies.

Now, the Queen had an only son, called Giovannino, of whom she was exceedingly proud, because he was the handsomest young man of all the country for miles around. A few days after this had happened,

Giovannino began to grow hair all about his hands and face, and shortly after all over his body. Then, instead of walking on his feet, he began crawling on all fours. In fact, he was turned into a nasty-looking pig.

You may well imagine the horror of the Queen when she saw this ! Weeping and sobbing, she ran to the fairies, and begged them to give the boy back his lovely features. But the fairies turned away murmuring incomprehensible words, and the Queen went back to the

palace more unhappy than ever, to find Giovannino all dirty and disagreeable because he had been wallowing in the mud.

Yet Giovannino knew all about his own fate, because a fairy godmother had come to him in his sleep and told him. He knew that,
unless a beautiful girl would fall in love with him and marry him, he
would remain a grubby pig to the end of his life. One day he went
wandering about in the country, and came to a mill where there lived
a miller with his three daughters, the prettiest in all San Fiaschetto.
On the doorstep stood the eldest, and Giovannino went up to her, but
the girl pushed him off, saying : " Get away, you dirty pig ! "

Poor Giovannino rolled down the steps, feeling very much
humiliated. A Prince to be treated like that by a miller's daughter !
When he arrived at home, he shut himself up in his rooms and would
neither eat nor drink for several days.

Yet after a while he made up his mind to try his luck again, and
back he went to the mill. The second daughter was sitting on the
steps, but when Giovannino came near she kicked him, crying : " Off
with you, you horrid pig ! "

This was very sad indeed for Giovannino, who began to think that
never, never in his life would he find a beautiful girl, not alone to marry
him, but even to look at him, and that he would have to remain a pig
to the end of his days. So he threw himself under his bed and would
not budge for a long time.

At last, out he crawled again, and went trotting along until he
came once more in sight of the mill. In the yard the youngest
and prettiest of the miller's daughters was very busy feeding the
chickens.

" If she kicks me, I'll kill myself and make an end of it," said
Giovannino to himself as he came nearer. He was looking rather unpleasant because, as there were several pools on the way from the palace,
he had been wallowing in the mud. Yet he pulled himself together,
and came very near little Firmina, who, instead of kicking him away,
said in a kind voice : " You poor little beast ! "

Giovannino, greatly encouraged, came nearer and whispered :
" Tell me, pretty miller's daughter, do you think you could love me ? "

" Yes, I could, poor little beastie," answered Firmina.

Giovannino at this answer felt bolder and bolder and stammered out : " Pretty miller's daughter, would you marry me ? "

" Yes, I would," replied the girl.

Then the Prince-pig, almost beside himself with excitement, took his bride back to the palace : his people were delighted to know that he had found someone to marry him, ugly as he was, and there was a beautiful wedding.

When Giovannino was left alone with his bride, all of a sudden he was turned into the handsome young man he was before the accident, and to the delighted Firmina he said : " I shall always be like this if, for three months, three days, and three hours, nobody knows anything about it and nobody but you sees me."

Of course Firmina promised that she would never whisper a word to anybody, and for two months they were very happy. But then people began to feel envious, because the miller's daughter looked ever so happy and so much in love with her husband, in spite of his being a pig, and they whispered that either Firmina had married just for the sake of being a princess and that she hated Giovannino for all that, or that there was some secret and that the Prince was not really always a horrid pig.

All this came to the ears of the Queen, who was already a little suspicious, and she felt very jealous because she was almost sure there was something her daughter-in-law knew and she did not. So she began to worry the poor little thing, and one evening she called her up to her and said :

" Tell me, miller's daughter, why did you marry my son ? "

" Because I loved him."

" Is it true, what I hear, that my son is at times changed into a fine young man ? "

" It may be so, and it may not be so."

" What is my son like when he is alone with you ? "

" That I cannot tell."

At this the Queen became more and more angry, and shouted out : " I'll see my son when he is asleep."

"A THOUSAND MILES AN HOUR."

From "The Quest of the Bird with the Golden Tail."

" That you shan't," said Firmina.

" You impudent little minx ! " cried the Queen, in a paroxysm of rage. " I'll teach you to answer a Queen like that ! I shall see my son whenever I please, whether you will or not. I am the Queen, and I alone command here. If you say one more word I'll have your silly head cut off."

" Very well," sobbed out Firmina.

So that night when Giovannino was asleep Firmina unlocked the door and let the Queen in, and when the Queen saw her boy so handsome and young she cried out : " Oh, my son, how beautiful you are ! " This woke up Giovannino, who was immediately changed into a bird with a fine golden tail, and he flew out of the window, saying to his wife : " In order to find me you must walk for seven years, wear out seven pairs of shoes made of iron, and fill seven flasks with your tears, when I shall be yours once more."

And off he flew, leaving a golden trail behind him.

The poor little miller's daughter sobbed her heart out when she realised that her Giovannino had really gone. But, remembering his parting words, she immediately procured for herself the seven pairs of iron shoes, and seven iron rods to lean upon on the way, and began her sad quest, willed by the fates. For months and months she travelled on, through mountains and plains, on stones and crags and rocks, tearing herself on thorny bushes, losing her way through unknown countries, asking everyone she met whether they had seen the Bird with the Golden Tail.   But nobody had seen him.

One day, when she had walked for nearly seven years, and used up all the shoes but the pair she was wearing, all the rods but the one she was leaning upon, and had cried and wept so much that all the seven flasks had been filled and she had no more tears to shed, because they were all dried up, she came to a dark wood, and in a dusky corner she saw a house.   A little old wrinkled woman was at the window, and Firmina called out to her : " Dear little woman, have you seen the Bird with the Golden Tail ? "

" I have not seen him, my dear.   Perhaps my husband has seen him, but you had better be off before he comes back, because he is an Ogre, and would eat you should he find you here.   This is the country of the Ogres."

" Pretty little Ogress, please let me hide in your house.   Perhaps I may hear where my Giovannino is, and also I am so tired that I cannot walk another step to-night."

The Ogress would not take her in at first because she was almost sure the Ogre would eat the poor little thing, and she felt so sorry for her. Yet after a while Firmina insisted so much that she was allowed to come in and was hid in an empty cask.

Presently the Ogre came home and began sniffing about.   " I feel there is something to eat here.   Where is it ? "

" There is absolutely nothing here, you old stupid," said his wife. " But some time this morning somebody came in and asked whether you had heard of a Bird with a Golden Tail."

" I know nothing about the Bird with the Golden Tail," growled the Ogre, " but I know there is something to eat in the house.   I smell it ! "   And taking a magic whistle out of his pocket, he struck up a tune, so that presently everything in the house began to dance and kick about, and fly here and there and everywhere.   You can imagine poor Firmina in the cask !   She was all sore and knocked about, yet she did not utter a cry ; and finally the Ogre, having satisfied himself that he could get hold of nothing to eat for the present, went to bed feeling cross and hungry, and early in the morning got up and went out hunting.

"EVERYTHING IN THE HOUSE BEGAN TO DANCE."

As soon as he was out of sight, the Ogress came up to the cask and let the girl out, saying kindly : " My poor child, I am so sorry for you : there you are, all sore and hurt, and yet you know nothing about your bird. Take this chestnut and open it when you are in need."

Off went Firmina, and all the day she roamed about in the wood, until at night she reached another house in a thick cluster of trees. Firmina knocked at the door and begged to be let in for the night.

" Get away as fast as you can, my daughter," answered the woman who came to the door. " Don't you know this is the country of the Ogres ? The wood is full of them. If Malfatto finds you here when he comes home, he will eat you on the spot."

" Dear little Ogress, I am looking for the Bird with the Golden Tail. If your husband is really an Ogre, he may know where the Bird is. Do let me in and have a chance."

The kind Ogress at last let the girl in, and hid her in a pair of the Ogre's shoes.

Presently Malfatto came in and began scenting the air.

" There is a human being in this house," he said to his wife.

" Don't you be an old idiot," cried his wife. " There is nobody in the house now, but this morning a girl came along and asked whether we knew of a Bird with a Golden Tail."

" I know nothing of the Bird with the Golden Tail," roared Malfatto, " but if I find something hidden here, I'll make you suffer for it." Pulling out a whistle, he began whistling until everything in the house was set going ; the chairs went up to the window-sill, the table hit the ceiling, and as for the shoes Firmina was hidden in, they went right up and then down again with a big thud on to the floor, so that Firmina thought she was going to die, and yet she had learnt nothing about Giovannino.

In the morning, after Malfatto had gone, his wife let the girl out and gave her a walnut, saying : " Open this when you are in need."

The little miller's daughter crawled out cautiously, feeling very weary and sad and sore. Yet she would not stop to rest, and at night she had reached another house at the very end of the wood. A hideous old hag was at the window, who, when she saw Firmina coming near, shouted in an angry voice : " Get off, you silly thing, or I'll hit you."

" Please, madam, tell me, have you seen the Bird with the Golden Tail ? "

" Get off, you and your iron shoes ! I know nothing of a Bird with a Golden Tail. I daresay my husband knows all about it, because he knows everything ; but you may have heard of Mangialupi. If he sees you he will eat you, iron shoes and all. Ha, ha, ha ! ! ! "

" Please, madam, please let me in for the night. I'd give anything for a chance of knowing where my little Bird has gone. Do let me hide in your house ! "

" All right, if you want to be eaten, come in," said the Ogress in a slightly less gruff voice. And pushing Firmina in, she hid her under a heap of rubbish and stones in a corner of the cellar.

At dusk Mangialupi came in, feeling very hungry and cross. As soon as he got to the house he began to sniff about and cry : " I smell some young meat."

" Be quiet, you silly," growled his wife ; " but you might tell me, you old wretch, where the Bird with the Golden Tail is."

" What do I know of your silly Bird ? Am I the King of the Winds ? Where did you hide that fresh meat ? "

And as his wife, instead of giving him information, scolded him like an old trooper, he took out a whistle and started the usual Ogre-tune. All the house went dancing about ; the chairs, the stove, the cupboards, the tables, everything went whirling around, as if shaken by a hurricane and a wind combined. Even the poor old Ogress was shaken about and thrown against the window-panes and up to the ceiling.

As for the poor little miller's daughter, who, as I have told you, was hiding in the cellar under a heap of rubbish and stones, you can easily guess how she was thrown against the walls and hurt by the stones that were supposed to hide her. By the time—and it was a long time ! —that Mangialupi grew tired and stopped whistling and everything had gone to rest, the poor child was terribly bruised, she was bleeding sorely. Fortunately, Mangialupi could not see her, and he went to bed growling like a cross bear with a very sore head.

In the morning the Ogress went to Firmina to say that, as the Ogre had gone out, she might as well take her chance and flee.   The poor old thing was very sore too, yet she seemed kinder towards the girl who was going through so much in order to find her lost love.

"Did you hear what Mangialupi said last night?   It is not the Ogres you must ask for news of your little Bird.   The only one who knows is the King of the Winds."

"Thank you, madam," cried Firmina, overjoyed at the thought of gaining information; "and pray tell me, where does the King of the Winds live?"

"See that highroad in the distance?   They all live over there. Now go, or you'll get me into trouble.   Here is a peanut for you. Open it when you are in need."

The miller's daughter thanked the Ogress, who after all, in spite

of her rudeness, had been so helpful to her, and ran along to seek the house of the King of the Winds.

On and on she tramped through forests dark and full of crawling beasts that filled her with fear, through swamps and marshes, through rivers she had to swim across, through thorns and prickly bushes that tore her hands and feet; but at last she arrived at the foot of the mountain on the top of which was the home of the Winds.

There she stopped for a few minutes, to get a little breath; then she began climbing the steep rocks, until at last she reached the top and stood before the open door of the stronghold, when a great gust of wind pushed her into a big vaulted room without any furniture, because all the furniture that there was had been smashed by the winds that blew in and out when and as they pleased.

"Please, kind Wind," said Firmina to the Wind that was shaking her about, "tell me where is the Bird with the Golden Tail?"

"I don't know, my child, but ask my brother the East Wind: he may know," and the Wind blustered out of the room. Presently Firmina felt that something was pushing her violently against the walls, and she felt the East Wind blowing in like a fury. But the East Wind knew nothing about the Bird, and went out very cross, shaking her, and making her feel chilly and sore.

Then the Southern Wind blew in very gently, and said that he knew nothing about the Bird, but that the North Wind was sure to know. Off he went, leaving Firmina on the floor, because, although he pretended to be so gentle and calm, yet he blew strongly all the same.

The North Wind rushed in all of a sudden, and the room became almost frozen, and the miller's daughter began shivering with cold. Blowing about so that the place was all shaken and poor Firmina quivering and quaking with cold fear, he asked in a gruff voice: "What do you want of me?"

"Kind Northern Wind, I want to get to the Bird with the Golden Tail."

"The Bird with the Golden Tail is thousands of miles away from here. Of course I know where he is—the Northern Wind knows everything: if you are not frightened, jump on my back and I will take you to the spot."

Firmina felt rather scared at the thought of going for so many thousand miles in the air on the back of a roaring Wind; but she did not say a word, and mounted bravely. The North Wind dashed out like a fury and darted off like lightning.

One moment he was tearing across the sea, the next he flew above the highest mountain of the earth, the following he was rolling in an abyss, up and down, here and there and everywhere, at the speed of a thousand miles an hour. The miller's daughter on his back felt that her skin was growing weather-beaten and withered, and that she was rapidly getting older and older and very ugly. How tired she felt! The North Wind was flying so fast that she could hardly breathe, and she felt that she could endure it no longer. At last the Wind slowed down, and after a short while put her down on a fine lawn, outside a beautiful house.

"See that beautiful castle? It is there where your little Bird lives, but I warn you that from to-day he is no longer a little Bird but a handsome prince. Now good-bye, and good luck to you!" and saying so he darted off to the North Pole, to see what had happened to his kingdom during his absence.

As soon as the miller's daughter had recovered a little of her breath, she went to the farm—she did not dare go to the front door of the house—and before she had time to say anything a man came out and asked in a kind voice: "What do you want, my poor little Grannie?"

Poor little Grannie, indeed! That was what she had come to, after so many years of suffering! How could she come to Giovannino, who was now a fine young man? He would never know her, the pretty little bride of seven years ago, and would have her thrown out of the house. Her eyes filled with tears, but she bravely kept them back and said to the farmer: "Please, kind farmer, I want some work to do."

"Very well," said the farmer; "we have just lost the girl who looked after the geese. If you like, you may take her job; I daresay it won't be too much for you."

So Firmina went to look after a big flock of geese, and when she came to a brook by a field she gazed at herself in the clear running water, and saw that she had been turned into an old hag, with a skin like that of a brown potato, ragged and dusty and slightly humpbacked.

"What is the good of my having done all this and gone through so much?" she cried in despair. "Now, even if I could see my

Giovannino he would never know me.   If only he were still a poor little pig as he was when I married him, it would not matter so much my being ugly.   But he is a handsome prince, and he will have nothing whatever to do with me."

As she was saying this, the geese began to cackle and shout : " Where is the chestnut ? "

Then Firmina remembered the chestnut that had been given her by the first Ogress, and she immediately opened it.   Out came a wonderful dress all made of silk of the finest texture, of the colour of the air, all embroidered with golden birds.   The miller's· daughter put it on at once, and suddenly all her wrinkles disappeared as if by magic, her eyes became shining and blue and bright, her hair was again like lovely golden silk, her hands were white and smooth ; in fact, she was even more beautiful than when Giovannino first met her at her father's mill.

When the geese saw this, they immediately began to cry : " Oh, how beautiful our mistress is !   How beautiful our mistress is ! "

At the noise made by the geese the old Queen, who lived in the castle and was trying to get Giovannino to marry her, came along.   The Prince had refused to marry her, first of all because she was old and wicked, and then because he still hoped that his Firmina would come and find him.   So old Nasturzia kept him a prisoner in the castle and would never allow him out.   Now when Nasturzia saw the beautiful dress she immediately wanted it, because she was as vain as she was ugly.

" You shall have it if you let me stay in the Prince's apartments to-night," said Firmina.

" All right, you shall be allowed in until the cock crows," replied the Queen, and she took away the dress.   But in the evening she ordered a sleeping draught to be put in the Prince's wine at dinner, so that he fell asleep in the dining-room and had to be carried upstairs. Shortly after, Firmina came in and she began to cry and say : " Seven strong pairs of shoes, all made of iron, have I worn out to come and find my love !   Seven strong rods, all made of purest iron, have I leant on in my journey to my love !   Seven flasks with tears, bitter tears, have I filled, in seven long, cruel years ; now I have found you, my love, my own darling, and you sleep on and will not heed my grief ! "

All night she went on like this, weeping sadly and trying to waken her husband ; but the draught was very strong, and Giovannino slept until the morning came and the cock crowed, and Firmina had to go back to her geese.

In the afternoon, when in the field, she opened the walnut, and out came a dress even more beautiful than that of the previous day ; and all the geese gathered around her once more, and cried out : " Oh, how beautiful our mistress is ! We never saw anything like that ! " And Nasturzia came out, and had the dress on the same condition. But again the Queen had the sleeping draught put into Giovannino's wine ; so, in spite of Firmina's tears and bitter cries, her husband slept on until the cock crowed, and she had to go.

The following day, Firmina opened the last nut, and oh, what a fine dress came out of it ! It had the loveliest hues of a beautiful Eastern night, and the moon and all the stars were embroidered on it. One could see it miles away, it shone so brilliantly ! Again Nasturzia had it, on the usual condition ; but the miller's daughter felt terribly sad, because it was her last chance, and if her Giovannino did not awaken that night, she would have to go away and be without him for ever.

But that night, before sitting down to dinner, Giovannino asked the cup-bearer : " Tell me, cup-bearer, why is it that the last two nights I fell asleep on the table ? "

" Mind the wine, Prince," answered the cup-bearer ; " and by the way, Prince, every night we hear moans and groans come out of your room. Do you hear anything ? "

" I have not so far, but I will take care," answered Giovannino. So that night, instead of drinking the drugged wine, he threw it under the table when nobody was looking, and went early up to his room. Presently Firmina came in, looking more beautiful than ever, but oh ! how sad ! And she began her tale : " Seven strong pairs of shoes all made of iron . . . " Then her husband knew her at once and took her in his arms and kissed her, and told her how he had been waiting and waiting for her to come and rescue him. Had she not come that very day to break the spell, he would have had either to marry old Nasturzia or be turned into a bird for ever.

In the morning Giovannino, radiant with happiness, took his pretty, faithful little wife downstairs with him. When Nasturzia saw her, she understood her power had gone, and, mad with rage and envy, she dropped dead on the floor. So Giovannino and Firmina remained sole rulers of the beautiful castle and of all the fine grounds around it.

A few days later Giovannino gave a great dinner to celebrate his

coming back to human life and the faithfulness of his darling bride. All the princes and kings of the countries round came to the feast, and everyone marvelled at Firmina's great beauty and gentle manners. And Giovannino and the miller's daughter lived happy for ever after, loving each other more and more every day.

Somebody saw them in the days of old,
And this is how the tale came to be told.

MALCONSEIL

FAR, far away, shining brightly under the rays of the Italian sun, stand the snowy peaks of the Alps, like wonderful, strangely shaped statues, clearly outlined in the bright blue sky.

The rocky surface, just below the eternal snows, is dotted with the loveliest flowers, perhaps sown by the angels, or the fairies after their midnight dances. You can see bright red rhododendrons, pale blue violas, the pink anemones and yellow alpine daisies that are only to be found by the ridges of the glaciers; and, perched in the most dangerous places, a defiance to those that would like to gather it, the white velvety edelweiss, the star of the snows.

Amongst these flowers and these rocks, looking like a sapphire fallen from the crown of Our Lady of the Snows, there is a little lake, whose waters are so clear, so deeply blue, that they say it is a bit of sky dropped there just by accident.

The small lake is far away from the villages : hardly ever a living soul is seen near it : only at times a wandering chamois comes to the banks to drink some of that pure water. Above, in the deep blue sky, an eagle flies, tracing great circles, looking for its prey.

The lake is so beautiful and calm, the landscape so wild and still, that it seems almost impossible for their peace ever to have been troubled. And yet those waters, as transparent as crystal, have a secret as deep and mysterious as themselves. This secret is known to the winds, who only tell it to the larches in the vast wood below, or to the Lady of the Snows, who sits on her throne higher up, between two rocks, very near the sky.

This secret I am going to tell you : I heard it whispered by the breeze one fine night that I was sitting on a stone by the lake, counting the falling stars and listening to the babble and chattering of a brooklet that ran away from the lake in a great hurry, impatient to reach the valley where men live, where so many strange things unknown to the mountain seem to be happening daily.

Long, long ago there was a little grey stone cottage surrounded by a small field on the hillside below the larch-wood. In the cottage there lived old Magna Martric and her son Renzo, the handsomest shepherd of the valley—tall, with jet-black hair that curled and waved, and dark brown eyes so full of light and mischief that once seen they could never be forgotten.

Renzo and his mother were quite well off : they had several sheep and goats, two cows, a pig, and numberless hens. Between the two of them they did all the work, and when Renzo went down to the valley to sell butter and cheese, the girls looked at his fine, tanned features, and said to each other : " Whom is he going to marry ? Happy and lucky will be his bride ! "

But Renzo was only eighteen and did not think yet of choosing a bride, although he liked girls, and especially the Mayor's daughter, a

pretty little thing, two years younger than he. She knew it, and had in her heart a very soft spot for the handsome shepherd. She always managed to be on her balcony, watering the flowers, she herself the sweetest blossom, whenever she knew that Renzo was going down to market. On every fine spring and summer day, Renzo used to take his sheep and goats up to the larch-wood ; and, while they grazed and roamed about at their own sweet will, he would lie on the soft, dry alpine grass, in the shade of a larch or under an alpine-rose bush, watching the falcons and the eagles describing their wonderful circles in the blue.

One fine August afternoon, when all the voices of the mountain were still, and he, on the grass as usual, was enjoying the cooling caress of the alpine breeze, he heard a wonderful sound in the air. It was a music that came from afar, sounding more like an echo than like a real voice—a song so sweet and tender, so full of harmony, that it could not be the expression of a mortal, but rather that of an angel.

Renzo listened, almost awe-struck, until the last note died away in the air ; then he rose and began to look here and there and everywhere, trying to discover the divine singer ; but he could see no one, not under the bushes, not in the shadows of the larches, and not amongst the rocks where were only the sheep, peacefully grazing, and the goats, climbing the most dangerous slopes—so dangerous, indeed, that it seemed as if they must fall from the heights and break their necks. But goats know how to guard against these dangers and escape without hurt.

That evening, when the Shepherd's Star shone bright above the snowy peak, Renzo took the usual path home, followed by his little flock; but, whereas ordinarily he was cheerful and bright and sang lustily some merry mountain song, to-night he looked annoyed and discontented, for he had not been able to find out who was the wonderful singer.

"What is the matter with you, sonny?" asked Magna Martric, gazing anxiously at him, while she poured the boiling milk into the black earthenware bowl.

Renzo helped himself to the newly baked brown bread, the home-churned butter, the honey, flavoured with the scent of all the alpine flowers;

he did not want to speak, but his mother was looking so anxiously
at him, and he had never kept a secret from her, so finally he told of
the marvellous music and of his fruitless search.

Magna Martric frowned. " Listen to me, sonny," she said; " you
are very young, and you do not know. Beware ! beware ! There is
some witchery about this. The Fantina has an eye on you. Do not
heed her, my son, do not heed her ! "

" Who is the Fantina, mother ? " broke in Renzo excitedly. " Oh,
do tell me ! "

" It is dangerous to speak while the magic is still in the air, my
son," said the old woman, instinctively lowering her voice. " I will tell
you when you are older. But always beware of the mysterious voices
of the Alps."

Nothing more was said. Renzo would never have contradicted
his mother, but her words made him all the keener to see the Fantina
and hear once more the magic voices.

Again the following day he sought, seeking wherever he could,
but still in vain. The mountain would not disclose her secret. Again
he searched far and wide, and yet again he heard the voice, but the
singer remained invisible and undiscovered.

Then Renzo grew sad and sorrowful, and when he went down to
market he forgot to sing his usual mountain ditties, and he did not
give so much as a look at the Mayor's daughter, who was watering a
pot of geraniums. The geranium died because it had been watered
too much, and the pretty girl wept all day and all night.

When Renzo went back to the woods, it happened one day that
he missed a goat, the finest of the herd ; and, running off to find it, he
climbed and climbed until finally he reached the banks of the lake of
which I have told you at the beginning of the story.

And there, suddenly, a divine melody struck his ears, and marvelling,
he gazed around to where on the opposite bank stood a girl of wondrous
beauty.

Fair as might be the maidens of the valley, not one had he ever
seen so lovely as this. Tall, slim, with glorious fair hair, so fair that
it looked like shining gold, rippling in wonderful curls almost to her

"'COME,' SAID THE LIPS OF THE FANTINA."
From "Malconseil."

knees: a mouth that resembled a red carnation, and big eyes, of such a blueness that, in comparison, both the sky and the lake seemed to have lost their hue. There she stood, loveliest of the lovely, smiling at Renzo, who gazed in ecstasy at the entrancing vision.

He longed to go to her, but that was impossible : the lake was too deep and wide, and he had no boat : he was almost crying with sorrow when the beautiful one stretched out a hand towards the waters and said : " Walk ! "

Miracle !—the water was immediately frozen, just as it would be in the middle of the winter. Its surface was like a large piece of glass, a path easy to tread.

" Come ! " said the lips of the Fantina, as she stretched out her arms to him.

Renzo was now completely fascinated. He forgot his mother's warning, the lost goat, the Mayor's daughter watering the geraniums, and he began to walk across the frozen lake.

When he was right in the middle, where the water is so deep that many people believe it reaches the centre of the earth, the ice suddenly vanished. Renzo was drawn through the deep waters by a mysterious force ; the Fantina also disappeared from the banks, and soon her beautiful white arms were round Renzo's neck, and she was kissing him, whilst taking him to the magnificent grotto where she had made her home, below the deeps. . . .

.   .   .   .

That evening the little flock had to go home all by itself, and in the happy little cottage sorrow came to dwell.

And on stormy nights, when the sky is black and, raised by the winds, the waters toss and foam, one can see a dark form sitting on a stone by the lake of the Malconseil (the Bad Advice), wailing piteously. It is the mother of Renzo calling back her lost son.

And once a year, on a fine summer evening, while the Shepherd's Star shines bright above a snowy peak, and the sky is reddened by the glow of the setting sun, if you look straight down through the clear blue waters of the Malconseil, you can see quite distinctly, far below, two young people, one fair, the other dark, and they are kissing each other.   It is Fantina and Renzo, who are still together—

> Young, fair, and happy as happy can be;
> And this is all the wind told to me.

THE LEGEND OF THE WHITE CHAMOIS

THERE is amongst the Italian Alps a wonderful mountain which stands higher and more beautiful than all the others in the neighbourhood, rising up to the sky in a mass of abrupt peaks and deep precipices ; fields of snow and ice ; slopes where only the hardy rhododendron and the chilly edelweiss grow ; and ravines through which the torrents leap from rock to rock, in a froth of marvellous silver foam, amongst which the sunbeams seem to be playing gleefully, turning it into a mass of iridescent colours.

The name of this wonderful mountain is Monte Tricorno, and on one of the summits, called the Ricco peak, there is a very large cavern in which are kept the most precious treasures of the world.

A crowd of small gnomes, the spirits of the mountain, clothed in garments that bear the colour of the grass in spring, with little peaked caps, jingling with the merriest, tiniest silver bells, are carefully keeping these treasures from the greed of the inhabitants of the valleys below, who often try to come up unseen and snatch something of those untold riches, so mysteriously guarded, so carefully hidden that no one on earth can say that they have seen them. Yes, clever and strong as the treasure-hunters may be, they never succeed in entering the treasure cove. And how one of them tried and failed I am about to tell you in this story.

On the Monte Ricco, happy amongst the beauties of the grand mountain scenery, breathing freely the alpine air scented with the sweet perfume of the wonderful alpine flowers, mistresses of the whole place, there lived once upon a time three beautiful nymphs, that dwelt next door to the gnomes in a small grotto whose walls were shining with the brightest crystal gems. These nymphs were the shepherdesses of the Monte Ricco, and their duty was to look after a herd of agile and swift chamois that had their home on the mountain and grazed happily on the slopes, defying men to come and chase them among the abysses and precipices so plentiful in those lovely sites.

The head of the herd was one of the finest animals you ever saw— a beautiful thing, as white as the snow when it first falls from heaven and lies on the topmost rock where no human foot treads : far swifter and quicker in flight than ever chamois was in all the Alps. This chamois had two wonderful golden horns which shone brightly and vividly in the sunshine, so that, whether he was going from place to place or whether he was standing still, those horns gleamed like a golden star, making him unmistakable even from far away.

Now all the inhabitants of the valley knew of this wonderful beast, and they also knew that he who should succeed in killing it would become the possessor of the treasures hidden in the caves of Monte Ricco. But they also knew this : the chamois could only be killed

"A CROWD OF SMALL GNOMES, THE SPIRITS OF THE MOUNTAIN."

by the first shot. If he were missed, and only wounded, his blood falling on the rocks or on the snows would grow at once into the flame-coloured rhododendron ; the Slatorog—for such was his name,— feeding then on the flower thus caused to blossom, would immediately grow much stronger and fiercer, and suddenly turning on the unhappy hunter would rend him.

Therefore, as you will readily understand, it was by no means an easy task, the killing of the Slatorog, and many a peasant who had set forth on the adventure had promptly retired in fear and trembling upon espying the magic beast against the horizon.

Yet great was the temptation, for the treasures of Monte Ricco bore a charm for the mountaineers ; and it so happened that one day, many many years ago, the handsomest young man in the valley decided to chance it, for his dearest dream was to lay the golden horns of the Slatorog at the feet of his lady-love, the handsome Piera, the fair daughter of the richest man in the valley. He was the finest shot in

the country for miles around, and had never been known to miss a chamois, although he had killed hundreds hunting them on the snow-ridged mountains.

Piera, to whom he confided his wishes, greatly encouraged him : firstly, because she felt exceedingly proud at the thought of her young admirer accomplishing such a feet ; and secondly, should he be success-ful, her father would no longer object to their marriage.

So, one fine day, having said his prayers and recommended his soul to his patron saint, Sandro went forth in quest of the famous beast, certain that his carabine, that had never been known to miss a shot, would prove a faithful friend.   And already in his mind he thought of the joy of Piera when he should lay at her feet the slain Slatorog and the treasures guarded by the gnomes in the depths of Monte Ricco.

It was very early in the morning; the day dawning in the east painted the tops of the mountains all rosy in the early light, but presently they shone like gold in the glory of the rising sun.   Sandro climbed higher and higher, far above the valley and the forests, until he reached the place where there are no more trees or bushes, only short grass and alpine flowers and rocks and snow ; and there, as he stood on a large stone, dazzled by the glorious sunlight reflected on the snows, he beheld Slatorog, standing on a peak not very far distant, his golden horns glittering in the wonderful light, a strange and tantalising twinkle in his eyes.

Sandro raised his carabine and aimed at the beast : that carabine had never failed him, and he felt sure of his prey.   But somehow his arm was not steady ; was it owing to nervousness, or was it bewitched ? Be that as it may, the shot was fired, but, alas! it did not pierce Slatorog's heart, it merely wounded the magic beast.

Then began the final deadly race, Sandro trying to hit the Slatorog before the animal had a chance of feeding on the flame-coloured rhododendrons that were blossoming everywhere on the rocks and the snows wherever a drop of his blood had fallen ; the Slatorog fleeing like the wind, so that he might outrun the hunter and stop a while to eat the powerful blossom before Sandro had time again to aim at him.

It was a dreadful race, from rocks to ravines that skirted frightful precipices, along the silvery waters of the deep alpine lakes, across the torrents that fell from on high with a roaring noise ; it was a hard-set race for life or death.

And suddenly the tops of the mountain disappeared under a big, dark cloud ; the air was heavy, just as if a storm were coming. For a while the Slatorog was hidden from the sight of the bewildered hunter, and, lo ! when the cloud lifted, Sandro perceived quite near to him, emerging from the mists, the handsome white chamois, tall and bold and frightful, for he had eaten the flame-coloured rhododendron and was now ready to stand up and chase in his turn. Then was Sandro seized with a dreadful fear ; there he was, alone on the mountain with the beast he had tracked, and which was now thirsting for vengeance. Below there was a precipice, thousands of feet deep, at the bottom of which rushed a torrent with a tremendous uproar. Sandro, blinded by the gleam of the golden horns, bewildered by the thought that he was alone with a bewitched beast which he had wounded and which was now savagely on his track, felt dazed and lost all sense of distance and of wariness : so it happened that, as he ran madly off, he lost his footing and, falling over the precipice, he

"HE BEHELD SLATAROG STANDING ON A PEAK."
From "The Legend of the White Chamois."

was carried away by the foaming waters of the torrent down below. . . .

The Slatorog then, wild with anger at having been robbed of his revenge, fled down the mountain side as far as the dwellings of men, followed by his entire herd and all the spirits of the mountain. In his fury was everything destroyed, so that there was not a cottage nor a garden left in all the country round.

This happened long long ago ; and the legend says that it will be seven thousand years before a fir-tree grows again on the waste and desolation caused by the raging Slatorog.

But out of the wood of the first fir-tree a cradle shall be made, and the baby who shall sleep in that cradle shall be given by the three nymphs, keepers of the herd of wild chamois on the Tricorno, power to kill the Slatorog and knowledge of the magic word which alone will give him the pass to the unknown and marvellous treasures that the small green gnomes are still watching and warding in the beautiful deep caverns of Monte Ricco.

But as fir-tree and baby have yet to be born,
The Slatorog still keeps his bright golden horn

LITTLE GOAT-FACE

THERE was once a peasant called Masaniello, who lived in a poor little cottage on a hill. Masaniello was married and had twelve daughters, but this was a great misfortune to him rather than a blessing, as both he and his wife were so poor that there was not one thing in the world that they could call their own but the cottage, which wasn't much to look at, and which they had built themselves when they were married. Father, mother, and children worked in the fields from morning till night, but this only just kept them alive. It was such an enormous, growing family, and they always felt hungry.

One hot summer day, when the sun was high in the sky and the air was so clear and everything so full of light that it hurt the eyes, Masaniello was very busy digging at the foot of the hill, close to a great cavern, very deep and dark. No one had ever entered this deep cavern, for strange noises came from it, and it had an evil name in the country. Now the sun was so burning hot that, after a while, Masaniello laid down his tools and sat for a moment's rest under the shade of a large poplar that grew close by; and as he sat there, he thought of his misfortunes, and how unlucky it was that he and his wife should have such a horde of children when they could hardly afford to keep one.

As he was thus meditating, a huge green Lizard, as big and as fat as a baby alligator, suddenly crawled out of the cavern and sat by him. The poor man was terrified and dared not move for fear of the beast eating him up; but the Lizard evidently possessed a kindly disposition, for it drew nearer to the man, saying in a rather sweet little voice:

" My dear Masaniello, you need not be frightened, for I have no intention of harming you : on the contrary, I came out to see whether I could be of any help to you."

As Masaniello heard this, he felt somewhat reassured that the Lizard was not going to eat him on the spot. Yet it gave him a dreadful fright to hear the beast speak, and, turning away so that it could not see him, he crossed himself and made horns with his fingers to frighten away the evil eye. Then he tried to pull himself together, and said to the Lizard in his politest tone :

" Madam, I am most delighted to make your acquaintance. It is indeed kind of you to want to help me. As a matter of fact, I have twelve children and do not know how to make both ends meet. That is my only trouble, and I should be very grateful to anyone showing me a way out of my difficulties."

Hearing this, the Lizard smiled. It was a lovely fat Lizard, and the green scales of its skin shone in the sun like beautiful emeralds : also it had the pleasantest smile; you could see its pointed face beaming with glee. It was a really beautiful sight. Yet Masaniello did not enjoy it as much as he should have done, for there was always that fear lurking in a corner of his heart that the beast was making fun of him, and was simply gaining time in order to get an appetite. But the Lizard spoke once more and said in the most soothing voice : " My dear good man, I know of all your troubles and, as I have said, I have come out of my cavern on purpose to help you. Please bring round your baby girl to-night, and I will take care of her and bring her up as if she were my own daughter."

Masaniello was absolutely thunderstruck when he heard this—so much so that he lost his balance and fell on the ground, which was very prickly, because it was full of thistles. But the Lizard gently picked him up and put him upon his feet, and then told him it wanted an answer at once.

The poor father did not know what to do. It is one thing to be needy, and quite another thing to give one's own child into the keeping of a strange Lizard that, for all he knew, might make a fine meal of it. And in his mind he was cursing the moment he had come to dig at the foot of the hill, the master who employed him, and the day he was born ; but the Lizard, evidently not liking to be kept waiting, cried : " My good man, stop at once thinking all those silly things in your foolish, brainless old head. You are not to discuss whether you are going to give me your daughter or not, for, as I have made up my mind to have her, you might as well try to stop the sun from shining or the rivers from flowing. You run home this very minute and bring the child back, or woe betide you and all your unlucky family."

Poor Masaniello saw that there was nothing, absolutely nothing, to be done, and as he feared the Lizard's wrath—for was it not a terrible beast ? and it lived in that ill-famed cavern—he ran home looking a picture of misery, so that his wife, who had come to the door to greet him, was quite taken aback, for Masaniello, though poor, was quite cheerful as a rule.

" What has happened, my dear ? " his wife exclaimed. " Have you lost your employment ? Have you hurt yourself ? Or is the ass dead ? "

Masaniello could only hang his head and be silent, he was so

terribly agitated. But at last his wife got the whole story out of him,
how the Lizard had come out of the dreadful cavern, and how it had
said that unless they gave it Verdeprato to keep, some awful harm
would happen to the whole family.

Aniella took quite a different view of the matter.

" Who can tell," said she, " that all this is not for our own and
for Verdeprato's good ? Who tells you that the Lizard is bad-natured ?
If it were, it would have eaten you when you were so rude to it. As

far as I can see, the Lizard is well-intentioned and means no harm to
our daughter.   Anyhow, if she stays with us, she can but die of hunger
some day or other, so we may as well take the risk."

These words greatly comforted Masaniello, who was in the habit of
always taking his wife's advice in everything.   So he went upstairs
and, with Verdeprato in his arms, soon arrived at the poplar tree, where
he found the Lizard patiently waiting for him to bring the child.   When
the beast saw that Masaniello had done according to its wishes, it was
very much pleased and gave him a huge bag of gold; then, placing
Verdeprato on its back, it said :

" I shall be both a father and a mother to the child, believe me,"
and saying this it vanished inside the deep, dark cavern.

Masaniello took the gold ; he had never seen so much money
in all his life, and he went home very happy, for the Lizard seemed
most kind, and that bag of gold would allow him to bring up his
daughters and give them a dowry, while he and his old wife would
not be left to starve.   I am sorry to say that there was great joy in the
home when Masaniello went back that night, and baby Verdeprato
was not missed, for there were eleven more children, and, when there
are so many, one more or less is not much noticed, especially when it
is very small.

So soon as the Lizard and Verdeprato were deep down in the
cavern, the baby was given milk to drink and put to sleep ; and while
she slept the Lizard carried her some distance away, right to the top of
the hill, and there it made a most beautiful house, a great country
mansion with lovely grounds, fine lawns, gardens full of flowers and
big shady trees.   There little Verdeprato was taken into a pretty room
all white and pink, with two nurses to look after her ; but the Lizard
never left her for a moment, and was always ready to give her whatever
she might want to play with, and to spoil her in every way.   So Verdeprato grew up in those lovely surroundings, dearly loved by the Lizard
and all the servants of the house, a happy, care-free little girl with marvellous green eyes (that is the reason why her parents had called her
Verdeprato, because she had eyes the colour of the grass, which is
indeed a very rare thing).

"THE KING CAME TO TAKE HIS BRIDE."

Time passed and the years went by : Verdeprato grew into a very pretty girl with gentle manners, for she was very well brought up. The Lizard she loved like a mother, and in this she was quite right, for the Lizard had been both a father and a mother to her, according to its promise.

Now it happened that one day the King of the country went out hunting, and he hunted so late that he ended by losing his way, and wandered around looking for a shelter for the night. As he was beginning to be distressed, for he could not find his way home and no house was in sight in that deserted place, he suddenly perceived a light shining on the top of the mountains, and immediately he sent his servant to ask who it was that lived there, and whether they could give their King shelter for the night.

Shortly afterwards the Lizard appeared, but not in the usual shape ; it was a tall, stately lady in a fine garment of silver and gold, followed by a number of servants, that came out to greet the King and to say how much honoured she felt at being able in a small way to oblige his Majesty, and at being his hostess even for one night.

The King, most delighted at this gracious welcome, followed the lady into the house, marvelling at the beauty of the gardens and the rooms. Upon arriving at the great dining-hall, a hundred pages came to meet him, while a hundred young girls were playing the softest, loveliest music. The dinner was served on gold plates, and it was one of the most splendid dinners the King ever sat down to. But what charmed him most in that magnificent place was the beauty and the grace of Verdeprato, who was there at the table beside her mother Lizard, who had kept the shape of a fine lady, and who showed herself as the most charming of hostesses.

As it was, the King, instead of going away the next day, stopped nearly a week in the beautiful house, and when he at last left, much against his will, he begged of the Lizard to allow him to make Verdeprato his Queen. The Fairy, who loved the girl more than if she had been her own child, and whose greatest wish was to see her well married, was delighted at this unexpected good fortune. So she said she would prepare everything for the wedding, and also that she would give

Verdeprato a dowry of a million pieces of gold, so that she should be well fitted to be a king's bride.

The next morning the King came to take his bride and bring her to the palace. But the ungrateful little girl, forgetting that, but for the kindness of the Lizard, she would have been nothing but a poor, half-starved little peasant, doing the roughest work without ever a moment of pleasure or rest, went off without saying as much as one word of thanks to the good Fairy.

The Lizard was deeply pained by such gross ingratitude, and in her anger and sorrow wished that the girl's face might become like that of a goat, so that she should repent of her ungrateful behaviour and come round to better feelings.

So it was that, when the King arrived at his palace and looked at his would-be bride, in-stead of the lovely face with the green eyes and the golden hair, he beheld an ugly, stretched - out mouth, hairy cheeks, and a long, coarse beard. You can easily imagine his astonishment and disap-pointment and anger at seeing this dreadful change ; he thought he had been the victim of some wicked spell, and exclaimed :

"I shall certainly not be the husband of a goat ; I cannot bear to see such an ugly sight ! " After which he sent Verdeprato to the kitchen and ordered a maid to look after her.

As the girl was so ugly, he thought that she might at least make herself useful, so he told her and the maid to spin ten bundles of flax, saying that it must be ready by the end of the week. The maid immediately began to work, and to work well ; but Verdeprato—who, by the way, did not yet know that her looks were changed, for there was no looking-glass in the room—began to grumble and say : " This is indeed a great shame, that I, the bride of the King, should be treated in this disgraceful fashion and sent to the kitchen to work in the company of a maid ! I shall certainly not do anything, I who have brought to the King such a splendid dowry," and she threw the flax out of the window, spending all her time doing nothing but make herself disagreeable to her companion. When the end of the week came and Verdeprato saw that the maid had spun all the flax, she began to worry and be afraid lest the King should punish her severely for having thus openly disobeyed his orders. So, not knowing how to get out of trouble by herself, she begged to be allowed to go out for a while, and ran away to the Lizard, telling her what had happened and begging her to let her have some spun flax. The good-natured Fairy immediately gave her some flax to prevent her being punished, but, as the naughty child ran off without even saying good-bye, the Lizard's feelings were hurt once more, and she did not break the spell.

When the King came round he was much pleased to see that the flax had been well spun, and he gave the two girls two little dogs to keep, saying that he would come back and see how they had looked after them in a week's time. The maid was very kind to hers, and gave it food and fresh water every day ; but Verdeprato, still as angry as ever, took hers and threw it out of the window.

As the week drew to the end, again Verdeprato began to be frightened as to what the King would say when he learnt the end of the poor little dog. Again she ran away from the palace and went to her good Fairy to beg her to get her out of trouble once more.

At the house gate stood the old porter, who, instead of letting her in, said in a rather gruff voice :

" Who are you, and what do you want here ? "

Verdeprato was furious at being addressed in this way, and she looked at the porter proudly, saying in a very rude manner :

" Why don't you let me in at once ? Don't you know me, you old goat-beard?" You can easily imagine how annoyed the porter was to hear himself called " goat-beard " by a girl who had a goat's face herself. (You remember, though, that Verdeprato did not know as yet that she had a goat's face, because in those days mirrors were expensive things, and she had been kept in the kitchen, where there was not a chance of seeing one), and he made up his mind to

punish the girl. So he went into the lodge and came back with a looking-glass.

"To think," he said, "that you of all people should call me 'goat-beard'! Just look at yourself, you ungrateful little minx! Remember all the good Fairy has done for you, all the beautiful things she gave you, how finally she crowned them all by marrying you to a King—you, a mere peasant's daughter. And instead of feeling grateful and showing some gratitude, you have taken everything for granted and have never even given the Fairy a kiss or a word of thanks when you left, for your silly head was turned by too many gifts and too much kindness. The Lizard has shed grievous tears through your base ingratitude. And now, to crown it all, you call names the oldest and most faithful servant in the Fairy's household!"

When Verdeprato heard all this, and saw her horrid goat-face in the mirror, she suddenly realised how wickedly she had behaved, and how kind it was of the King to allow her to remain in the palace instead of having her thrown out into the streets to beg. Very humbly then, and with tears running down her cheeks, she begged of the old porter to let her in, so that she might go to the Fairy and tell her how deeply sorry she felt for all her naughty doings. Of course the porter, who really was a kindly old man and was very fond of the girl, let her in at once, and the Fairy, who had heard everything, came to meet her, thinking the child had been sufficiently punished. As soon as Verdeprato saw her benefactress, she threw herself at her feet sobbing: "Dear, good Fairy, please forgive me. I am so sorry, so sorry indeed!"

Then the Lizard touched the girl's face with a magic wand she was carrying, and suddenly changed Verdeprato into the beautiful girl she was before she had been so thoughtless and thankless.

After this they both entered the house, and once there the Lizard ordered the maids to dress Verdeprato in a lovely satin gown she had prepared on purpose; then a white veil all hand-embroidered was placed on the girl's head, so that her beautiful hair shone through like gold. Then, each mounted upon a fine horse, Verdeprato's as white as snow, the Lizard's as black as night, together they rode, followed by many servants, to the town and came before the King's palace, while

"ONE OF THE FINEST WEDDINGS YOU EVER HEARD OF."

everybody on their way strewed flowers before them, so that all the streets were carpeted with the most glorious blossoms, and the people shouted :

"Long live our Queen! How beautiful the King's bride is! May they live happy for ever!"

The King, who had been worrying himself greatly, not knowing what it was that had taken his pretty bride away from him, hurried to meet them and was more delighted than anyone can tell. With his whole heart he thanked the good Fairy for all she had done for them both, and then they entered the palace, where things were already being made ready for the wedding.

Then took place one of the finest weddings you ever heard of ; and all the gay people at Court danced and danced and danced so much that they were all so tired they had to sleep for a month to recover.

Verdeprato and the young King lived happy for ever after in the beautiful palace, made even more beautiful by the kind Lizard, who now and then came down to make lovelier their surroundings with her magic wand. Verdeprato never forgot the lesson she had so hardly learnt, and from her wedding day she always remembered to be grateful for all the things that were done for her.

As to Masaniello and his eleven remaining children, they lived wonderfully happily in a fine wooden hut that the Lizard had made for them.

As time went on the family increased, and soon the old people were surrounded by a huge family of children and grandchildren ; but there was always room in the cottage, for, as it was made by magic, so it became wider with every new arrival. And so the family, by working, but not too hard, and being very healthy and in need of nothing, felt they were the happiest people in the world.

Ever since those days lizards have always been held in high esteem by the peasants in the country, and woe betide him who would try to kill a lizard! They are considered the dearest of wild creatures, and are revered by all in remembrance of the Lizard of the Magic Grotto and of the happiness of Masaniello and his twelve children.

LUCIELLA

A LONG time ago there lived in a small cottage in the Alps an old woman
called Zia Marianna, who had three daughters, named Anna, Marta,
and Luciella.   While Zia Marianna's husband was alive they all managed
to get along quite well, for they had a field, two cows and a goat, besides
a small cottage, and Zio Piero worked hard from morning till night.
But when he died, which was a few years before the beginning of this
story, things began to go badly, there was no one to do the work, and
Zia Marianna was getting too old for spinning ; so little by little the field
was sold, then the cows, and after that the goat ; only the cottage was
left, with a tiny scrap of a garden where there was about enough room

for two cabbages to grow at the same time. And there was nothing much for the family to do but to get some odd jobs and go a-begging in the streets.

Anna and Marta, the elder daughters, were the laziest and the most unpleasant girls that ever lived, and they always tried to avoid doing anything for their mother. Also they were exceedingly jealous of Luciella because she was very beautiful indeed, for her teeth were like pearls, her lips like coral, her eyes were bright as the black diamonds, and as to her hair, it was just like flowing spun gold. She looked so lovely, in spite of her rags, that even the peasants, who generally do not bother much about personal appearance, would turn round to look at her as she went through the streets, and they were always glad to give her some odd fruit or vegetable to take back home. This, of course, made the sisters most furiously jealous, so that they were very unkind to her and always beat her whenever they got a chance.

One fine morning, as the sun was shining bright over the top of the hills, and the chestnut trees looked as if they were made of gold, for it was the autumn and the leaves were changing colour, Luciella came home, bringing her mother a beautiful large cabbage that had just been given to her by a peasant whom she had helped to push a cart up the steep hillside road. Zia Marianna was delighted, and said that she was going to cook it for dinner together with some onions she had, and it would give them all a treat. But when it came to putting the precious vegetable into the pot they discovered that there was no water in the house.

Said Zia Marianna to her eldest daughter : " Anna, be a good girl and go to the fountain to fetch some water."

Now the fountain was about half a mile distant, and there was a tiny, stony, steep path leading to it, so that it was always a matter of quarrel as to who should go to get water. Said Anna to Marta : " Now, you go and fetch the water ; " and Marta replied : " No, *you* go ; " and so on, until they began to quarrel badly. Then Zia Marianna, seeing the ill-will of her daughters, sighed deeply :

" Ah me, that a feeble, tired woman should be made to do such work in her old age ! For I see that there is nothing for me but to go myself and be the servant of my daughters."

So saying, she took up the pail and went out of the cottage door ; but hardly had she gone twenty steps when Luciella, who was in the field close by, helping some neighbours to pick up the fallen chestnuts, saw her, and at once ran towards her, took the pail, and went up to the fountain. Zia Marianna was delighted and returned home whispering : " God bless you, my child."

As for the sisters, they were quite annoyed and went on muttering in a corner.

Meanwhile Luciella, the pail on her arm, had climbed the path and reached the small fountain that sprang lightly out of a rock on to a green bed of soft, velvety moss. As the girl bent down to fill the pail, she saw a man-slave standing beside her, who said :

" Pretty girl, come with me. My master wishes you to come to his house, for it has been willed by the fates that you should marry him." Luciella, who had never been spoken to kindly in her home, thought it would be rather nice to follow the kindly slave, and, too, if things were willed by fate it was no use her saying yes or no. So she said she would just run home and take the pail, and that she would be back again in a minute.

Luciella soon returned again, and the slave led her along a hidden path amongst the fern under the chestnut trees, and after a while they came to a lovely grotto, overgrown with maidenhair ferns and creepers, which they entered. At the end of the grotto there was an underground passage made of glass, and through this they passed. When they had nearly reached their destination, the slave told Luciella that she was to be married to someone very rich and handsome and noble, but that the fates had willed that she should not see her husband for three years and three months, otherwise great harm would happen to them both. Luciella said that she was ready to do anything she was told, and presently they came to a magnificent palace, whose walls were made of shining gold, and the furniture of silver inlaid with diamonds and rubies. On the floor were costly Persian carpets and couches with most beautiful coverings. As Luciella stared in wonder, the slave clapped his hands and two lovely maidens came along, who took Luciella into an even more wonderful room. Here her rags were taken off, and she was dressed in fine silk and velvet, her beautiful tresses having first been combed; then they took her into the first room, where the slave again clapped his hands, and there appeared a table laid with the daintiest dishes; and poor Luciella, who was used to feeding on stale vegetables, had a meal such as she had never even dreamed of.

When she had finished she was taken to yet another apartment and told that the room would be darkened and then her husband would come in, but she was not to get any light to try to see him, for they were under a spell, and should she do so great harm would come to them both. Otherwise they would be happy, and wonderful things would happen to them later on.

And so they lived for several months, the mysterious husband only visiting her when it was dark, and the rest of the time Luciella played and slept and enjoyed herself generally, always attended by the slave and the two maids.

But it happened one day that she felt homesick, and began weeping. The slave at once came to ask what was the matter, and upon her telling him she wanted to see her mother and sisters, he went to his invisible master, and presently coming back gave Luciella a bag full of gold, saying : " The master is willing for you to go and visit your sisters, and sends them this money. But remember that you must not say a word about anything here, and never tell them what has happened to

"THE WITCH . . . HELD THE CRYSTAL UP TO THE FIRE."

you since you left them." So Luciella went off gaily, with the slave attending her as far as the fountain. It was late autumn now, the trees were bare and the tops of the mountains were covered with snow that shone dazzlingly in the sunshine. Luciella was very glad once more to see the hills and the sunshine and the blue sky. And especially she was glad to think that she was going to see her mother and give her all the gold.

Presently she arrived at the cottage and, running in, found Zia Marianna, Anna, and Marta sitting disconsolately round a fireless grate. Luciella kissed them and gave them the money ; but when they began questioning as to what had happened since she left them she remembered the slave's warning and only said she was very, very happy, that was all. After a few hours she wished them good-bye and ran away, followed by the slave, who had been waiting all the time at the fountain.

The wicked sisters were exceedingly annoyed at this good luck of Luciella's, and they tried to sharpen their wits and guess what might have happened. They were very angry, too, because Luciella had refused to say where she lived and who her husband was. As a matter of fact, she did not know much about it herself! As they could not guess anything themselves, they decided that they would take counsel with an old witch who lived on the top of the mountain and had a most evil reputation throughout the country, owing to her taste for young and tender children.

Up climbed Anna and Marta, heedless of the snow that was covering all the landscape with a white mantle ; and as they reached the top of the mountain they called out to the witch, who came out and was very much pleased when she saw them, for they were about as wicked as she was herself, and they liked plotting together as to how they could do harm. Together they went down into a strange room hung with the skins, horns, and claws of various beasts. There in a corner was a large brazier, and on the fire a big cauldron, beside which sat a huge black cat whose green eyes were like big lanterns. In another corner there were some flame-coloured and black books.

Then they all sat on the floor, and Anna told the witch of Luciella's good fortune, and how they wished to put an end to it. Upon which

"HE BENT DOWN TO KISS THE LITTLE BABY."
From "Luciella."

the witch, get-
ting up, put
some herbs to
boil in the cauld-
ron, and taking
one of the books,
and a crystal,
when the herbs
boiled she gazed
at them through
the crystal, and,
after studying
the book, she
held the crystal
up to the fire.

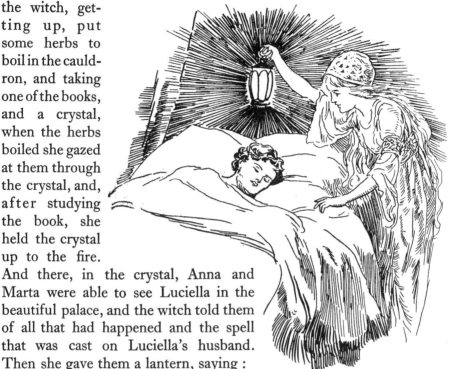

And there, in the crystal, Anna and
Marta were able to see Luciella in the
beautiful palace, and the witch told them
of all that had happened and the spell
that was cast on Luciella's husband.
Then she gave them a lantern, saying :
" When your sister next comes to
you, give her this lantern and tell her to look at her husband at night
when he is asleep ; tell her that this will break the spell and make
them both extremely happy. Then your wish will be fulfilled, for
her happiness will be destroyed for ever."

Anna and Marta were delighted at the thought of knowing all
about Luciella and of being able to put an end to her happiness. So
they bade the wicked creature good-bye and climbed out of the cave
holding the lantern safely in their hands.

When next poor little Luciella came to see them—and this time she
had brought them some lovely dresses, besides another bag of gold—
her sisters took her into the kitchen and said :

" Our darling sister, we have been worrying ever so much about
you, for we have discovered that, unless we can avert it in some way,

your husband will do you great harm. The only means to save you
is for you to look at him when he is asleep ; so we have procured this
lantern for you. All you have to do is to hide it under your pillow, and
at night, when you are sure he is asleep, pull it out and say : ' Lantern,
burn up,' and your husband will then be unable to harm you. You can
see how great is our love for you, as we have gone to all this trouble
to save you."

When poor, kind-hearted Luciella heard this, she gratefully thanked
the two sisters and went out, carrying the lantern under her cloak.
On arriving at the beautiful palace, she hid the ill-fated object beneath
her pillow as she had been told, and in the middle of the night took it
out, saying : " Lantern, burn up." Then it, being bewitched, came
alight, and in the dazzling light she saw her husband's face. The
lantern threw out a drop of burning oil which fell on the young
man's shoulder, and, awaking with a start, he found Luciella gazing
at him in admiration.

" Oh, why have you done this ? " he cried in a mournful voice.
And at that moment everything vanished from sight, and Luciella
found herself sitting on the snow, dressed in the rags she wore when she
first left the cottage, hugging her little baby close to her breast—for I had
forgotten to tell you that a dear, tiny baby had been sent to her a little
while before this happened.

There was the poor little thing, shaking with cold and with fright,
in a place unknown. Holding the baby close to her, she went about,
wandering in the snow and the ice, until at last she found her cottage
home ; but the wicked sisters beat her cruelly and sent her away.

For days and days Luciella and the baby went about shivering with
cold, living on the charity of passers-by, which was not much. She
wandered up and down the country, until one evening, when she was
so tired and ill that she thought she was going to die, she reached the
Queen's palace and fainted on the doorstep, her baby still held tightly
in her arms. Presently one of the Queen's ladies-in-waiting happened
to come out, and she took pity on the beautiful girl and the tiny babe,
so that she had them both brought up to her bedroom, where there
was a splendid fire. The baby was given some milk, and Luciella

too, and they were both put to rest in a warm, cosy bed, such as they
had not had for a long, long time.

Luciella was indeed very ill, and the kind lady watched her and
nursed her, being with her every moment she could spare. And so
it happened that one night she saw a handsome young man come into
the room, who, going to the cradle, took the baby up into his arms,
saying :

"Oh, my pretty darling little one, if only my mother could know
you, she would bathe you in a bath of gold, and she would swathe you
in bands of gold, and if the cock would never crow, I should never have
to go." But just as he said this, the cock began to crow and the young
man immediately disappeared.

The same
thing happen-
ed for several
nights, and the
lady - in - wait-
ing became
very much ex-
cited over it,
and finally
made up her
mind to tell
the Queen.
The Queen,
greatly aston-
ished, said that
she would get
to the bottom
of the matter,
and ordered
that all the
cocks in the
town should
be killed that

very same day. To the people of Torre Lunga this order appeared
somewhat cruel, yet, as it was the Queen's behest, there was nothing to
do but to obey, for otherwise the penalty would have been heavy. And
in the night, when all the stars were glittering and sparkling in the blue
mantle of the sky, the Queen went up to the room where Luciella and
the baby were, and she took the lady-in-waiting's place by the bedside.

   She had not been there many minutes when suddenly there appeared
the handsome young man. The Queen looked on eagerly and, as he bent
down to kiss the little baby, from a mark the young man bore on his
neck, she recognised him for her one and only son.

   Now you must know that when this son was born the witch that
had done Luciella so much harm, wishing to revenge herself on the
Queen, had cast a spell that the boy should never be seen by anybody,
and that he should disappear from the royal palace and lead a hidden
and desolate life until the day when his mother, to break the spell, would
kiss him without the cock crowing.

   So the Queen, finding in the strange young man the dear son whom
she had sought in vain for many many years, fell upon his neck and kissed
him ; and, as all the cocks in Torre Lunga had been slain on the previous
day, all was well ; the spell was broken and the Prince once more returned
to normal life. You may easily imagine the joy of the Prince who found
at the same time his mother, his wife, and his little baby ! As for
Luciella, her happiness was boundless, and from that day all her
troubles ceased, for she was safely guarded against all evil.

   When the wicked sisters heard through the infuriated witch how
Luciella had finally come to such good fortune, they actually had the
brazenness to come round to the palace and ask to see their sister. But
this time they could do no harm, much as they might have wished it ;
for the King ordered the two wicked ones to be taken, bound, and thrown
into a dungeon to meditate upon their sins.

   And so it came that Luciella and her King-husband lived happy for
ever after, their son becoming one of the handsomest and bravest princes
that was ever seen, and

> They were all so happy and bright
> That the witch burst with despite.

VIOLA

LONG, long ago there lived in Sicily three beautiful sisters, called Rosa, Garofana, and Viola. But, lovely as the two elder girls might be, the youngest, Viola, surpassed them greatly in beauty, being in comparison to them just what the evening star is to the other stars in the sky. Her sisters knew this, and were very jealous in consequence.

The three girls used to sit daily on their balcony, a pretty stone balcony, embowered with jessamine and roses; there one would spin, the other weave, and the third sew. Thus they spent their time, talking with each other, and dreaming of the man who would marry them.

One fine morning, as the King's son passed by, he looked at the flower-laden balcony, and was so dazzled by the three girls' beauty that he called out loudly to his cavaliers :

" Look, look at the priceless gems of my father's realm ! The one who spins is lovely ; she who weaves is lovely too. But she who sews is the loveliest of all and the Queen of my heart."

Having said these words he rode off, followed by his Court, and they all went hunting in the woods. But Rosa and Garofana were very much annoyed that he should have taken more notice of Viola than of them, so that the next morning Rosa, who was the eldest, made Viola sit at the spinning-wheel, and sat sewing herself, hoping that the Prince would say she was the loveliest. But as the Prince passed by and looked up at the pretty balcony, espying the three sisters diligently working behind the sweetly scented roses, he said :

" Beautiful is she that sews, and beautiful is she that weaves, but most beautiful is she that sits with such grace at the spinning-wheel." When she heard this, Viola blushed with pleasure at such notice being taken of her, for already she had fallen in love with the Prince ; but Rosa and Garofana were furious, and tried hard to think of some way of doing Viola harm to revenge themselves.

The third day they were again sitting at the usual place, and again the Prince came up the road as he was about to go a-hunting in the wood. This time Viola was made to weave in the background, whereas Rosa and Garofana, decked in their prettiest and smartest dresses, sat in front, smiling as sweetly as they could. (Their smile never could be very sweet, for they were too envious and too wicked for that.) In spite, however, of all this arrangement, the Prince passed by, saying : " Pretty is the one that spins, and pretty the one that sews, but the little gentle one that weaves so gracefully in the background, she is the prettiest, and she has won my heart."

After this, Rosa and Garofana were very angry and could bear this state of things no longer, so they thought of a horrid plan to get rid of their younger sister.

In those days thimbles were very precious and rare, and Viola possessed one that had been brought to her by her father from a far-away

"THE PRINCE PASSED BY AND LOOKED UP AT THE PRETTY BALCONY."

land. It was a beauty, made of gold, set with rubies and diamonds. Viola cared more for it than for anything else she possessed, and her sisters knew it. So they took it and threw it from a high window into a garden at the back of the house. It was a marvellous garden full of all the loveliest flowers ; there were palm groves, and orange and lemon blossoms that filled the air with the sweetest perfume, mimosas, jessamine, and roses, and all sorts of flowers and trees. But the garden belonged to a wicked Ogre that was known for miles all round the country for his taste for young and tender girls.

After throwing down the thimble, they went back to the balcony and asked Viola to do some sewing for them, so Viola rose to fetch her thimble, and felt very much distressed, for she could find it nowhere ; and as she was looking everywhere in the house, and not finding it,

Rosa called out to her and said :

" I'll tell thee what, sister mine. I'll have a look into my magic mirror; perchance it will tell me where the thimble has gone."

Viola thanked her gratefully, and then wicked Rosa ran upstairs and came back presently saying :

" Oh, Viola ! the thimble has fallen into Bruttaccio's garden— so the mirror says. But if thou wilt recover it, Garofana and I will tie a rope round thy waist and let thee down, so that thou canst get the precious thing, and we will pull thee up before Bruttaccio awakes from his afternoon nap."

Viola was quite willing to do anything she was told to recover her lost treasure, so Rosa and Garofana tied round her waist a very long rope and began letting her down. But, just before her feet reached the ground, they cut the rope, and the poor child was landed hopelessly in the Ogre's garden. It was absolutely impossible for her to escape, for she was surrounded by high walls made of glass, and no such thing could be even dreamed of. Yet the garden was so beautiful that Viola forgot the danger she was running, and instead of hiding she began wandering about the paths, marvelling at the wonderful flowers, hoping to be in time to hide behind some bush should she hear Bruttaccio coming along. But all of a sudden a horrible creature emerged out of a coppice wood, a hideous thing with strong, hairy arms like a monkey's, bristly hair of a bright crimson hue, and one eye twinkling right in the middle of his fore-head. Poor little Viola was so scared at this sight that, forgetting all precaution, she yelled out : " Mamma mia ! che orrore ! Aiuto ! " (" Mother mine, how horrible ! Help !"). As he heard this, Bruttaccio came forward, and, as he saw Viola, his very first thought was to eat her for his supper. But the girl looked so pretty and young that it seemed rather a shame that she should come to such an end, and besides she was somewhat too thin for his taste ; so he decided there and then that he would keep her as his daughter and maid-servant until she should be fat enough to make a really tasty dish.

Poor little Viola could not possibly know Bruttaccio's feelings towards her, and you may easily imagine how scared she felt. But after a while, as she saw how kind the Ogre was to her and how well she was treated (as a matter of fact, Bruttaccio was far kinder to her than her sisters had ever been), she was much pleased and did all the work there was to do cheerily, laughing and singing as she went to and fro about the house. Then it happened that one morning, as she was at the window doing her hair, a green and red parrot that belonged to the Prince, whose palace was not far from Bruttaccio's house, came along and, sitting on the window-sill, began laughing at the girl, saying :

> "Hugh, hugh, hugh ! "
> Bruttaccio will make a big meal of you ! "

Viola was very angry ; she ran in and told the Ogre, who said :

" Well, my dear, the only thing to do is to go back, pull the parrot's tail, and say :

> ' Parrot, parrot green and red,
> With the feathers from your head
> I shall make a cosy bed,
> And your master I shall wed.' "

Viola did as she had been told, and the parrot was so angry at being spoken to like this and having his tail pulled that he died in a fit of rage. The Prince, seeing that his parrot did not come home, went out and bought another, which came along to Viola's window as the first one had done and began laughing at her. But Viola answered him as she had answered the first one, so that this parrot also died from anger.

When the Prince saw that his second parrot had died, or at least had not returned to the palace, he was greatly vexed. Out he went and bought a third bird, determined to follow it wherever it went, so that he might see what happened and how the birds all disappeared. So he tied a long string to the foot of the parrot and kept the other end in his hands. Thus he was able to see the parrot go to Viola's window, laugh at the girl, and say :

> " Hugh, hugh, hugh, hugh !
> The Ogre will make a fat meal of you ! "

Then he recognised Viola for the beautiful girl he had fallen in love with when she was sitting on her balcony and he passed by to go a-hunting in the forest, and his joy was great, for he had tried in vain to find her, because in spite of all seeking nobody had been able to say what had become of her.

You can easily imagine Viola's joy when she saw the Prince, with whom, as I have already told you, she was very much in love. As the Ogre was sleeping at that moment, the Prince came as near as he could, so that they could talk without having to shout, and they decided that

"THEY RODE OFF QUICKLY."
From "Viola."

the best thing for them to do was to run away and get married, for they both knew by now that the parrots had been saying the truth, and that Bruttaccio was determined to make a meal of Viola at the first opportunity. Only it was very difficult to escape without the Ogre knowing it, for he slept with his one eye open, and always knew when something was moving about in the house.

"I'll go into the forest and ask my godmother to help us," said the Prince after a while. So, having said good-bye to Viola, he rode

into the forest, where the Fairy Merlina lived in the trunk of a large oak, and asked of her :

" Mamma Merlina, pretty Viola has fallen into the hands of Bruttaccio. What can I do to have her safely back with me ? "

Then Merlina went inside the oak to consult the Book of Words, and presently came out, holding a distaff, a clew of thread, and a comb. These she gave to Prince Lionello, saying :

" When you are in danger of Bruttaccio catching you, throw first the distaff, then the clew of thread, and finally the comb, saying at the same time : ' Merlina, Merlina, come and help us ! ' and all will be well."

Lionello thanked his fairy godmother and kissed her hand, after which, having carefully put away the charms, he rode back to the town. It was a lovely moonlight night, and all was silent in the streets, so he went up to Viola's window, where Viola was already waiting anxiously for him, and he said to the girl :

" Come down at once and let us run away before Bruttaccio wakes. Merlina has given us a charm that will save us should he run after us."

So Viola took up the rope by which Rosa and Garofana had let her into the Ogre's garden, and she tied it to a shutter and let herself down. When she reached the street Lionello took her into his arms, put her on his horse, and they rode off quickly. But unfortunately Bruttaccio knew at once what was happening, for he saw their image in a moon-beam, and, very angry at the thought of having been baffled and of losing a tasty meal that he had been looking forward to for such a long time, he sprang on his horse, a strange beast with five legs and no tail.

Soon Viola and Lionello heard the sound of the horse's hoofs behind them and became very much frightened, for Bruttaccio was almost overtaking them. But the Prince threw the distaff over his shoulder, crying: " Merlina, Merlina, help, help me ! " And all of a sudden the country between them and Bruttaccio became full of pointed swords, with point upwards, so that the Ogre could get on very slowly and hurt himself badly, while the two lovers galloped on. Un-fortunately, as soon as Bruttaccio had passed the swords he began to gallop too, and as his horse had five legs it ran much faster than Lionello's, which had only four, and again the lovers were about to be overtaken, when Lionello threw the clew of thread, crying: " Merlina, Merlina, help me ! "

And immediately there came between them and the Ogre a large stream of fast-running waters. But Bruttaccio forced his horse into it, and in spite of the current they managed to get through. Lionello and Viola were frightened almost to death when they saw him emerge, drenched and panting, out of the waters, for they knew he must be very hungry and cross, and that he would easily make two morsels of them both. Yet they did not lose heart and went on galloping, after throwing the last charm they had left, the comb.

And suddenly there came a very high mountain all made of soap between the Ogre and them—a steep, peaky mountain which it seemed impossible to overcome. Yet the lovers kept on galloping, turning round at every minute in fear of seeing Bruttaccio's ugly head appear on the top of it. But as the Ogre came to the foot of the mountain, much as he tried to make his horse climb it, he could not do so, for it was far too slippery and the horse kept falling down. Then he tried to climb it himself, but he kept on slipping and falling until at last he fell so badly that he broke his neck and died.

When the Prince and Viola saw that the danger was over, they were greatly pleased and went back to the palace, and there was a wonderful wedding, to which all the people in the country for miles round were invited, except, of course, the two wicked sisters, who had to be punished for their horrible behaviour.

As to Lionella and Viola, they lived happily for ever after under the protection of the Maga Merlina.

> They lived in bliss till a hundred years old,
> And so my story is said and told.

THE CHILD OF THE MYRTLE TREE

IN the bygone days there lived near Amalfi a woman called Cianna, who had been blessed with seven sons. They all lived very happily together, but their great wish was to have a sister, for, they said, there were already too many boys in the family, and they needed a girl to look after them and keep house for them later on. Yet wait and wait and wait, much as the mother desired it, no little girl came to the home, and this made them all feel very sad.

One day an old woman passed by and begged to be given some bread, for she felt very hungry. Cianna immediately came out to the door and brought bread and cheese. When the old woman had eaten it, she said: "What can I do for you, my good woman? Is there anything you specially wish for?"

"There is one thing I should like above all," answered Cianna, "and that is to have a little girl."

Then the old woman gave Cianna a small myrtle tree, saying : " Water this tree every day with the waters of a magic spring your sons will find in the wood of Selvascura. In a month, a little girl will be born to you."

Both the mother and sons were exceedingly pleased at this. They carefully put the tree in a beautiful pot, and the boys all started for Selvascura to get the water that was to give them their dearest wish. As they came to the forest, they looked everywhere, but could find no fountain. So they went one this way and one another, thinking that they were more likely to find it thus. All of a sudden Gennariello, the youngest boy, saw a beautiful white stag standing in front of him.

" Is it the magic spring you wish for ? " asked the stag.

" Yes," answered Gennariello, amazed to hear the beautiful beast speak. " Could you tell me where it is ? "

" Of course I can, and I will bring you to it, if you only promise to come back to me after you have taken the water home," was the reply. " I certainly will," said Gennariello. And the stag led him through an almost invisible path to a beautiful spot where the wood was thickest, where the poplars, the oaks, the chestnut trees, and the beeches joined overhead their marvellous foliage, so that one could hardly see through it glimpses of the bright blue sky. On the ground, in a small shrine of moss, maidenhair and other ferns, lay a shell of the most delicate pink hue, and in this shell were a few drops of the clearest water.

" This is the water you are seeking," said the stag; " you shall have it if you promise to come back to me as soon as you have taken it home, without saying a word of what you have seen to anybody."

Gennariello promised, and, taking the water in a little cask he had brought, went home, gave the water to his mother, and then ran back without telling anybody what had happened to him. As he came to the wood he found the stag waiting for him at the place where they had met in the morning.

" Follow me," said the stag.

When they had walked for a long time they came to a grotto in a

MORTELLA AND HER SEVEN BROTHERS.
From "The Child of the Myrtle Tree."

dense part of the forest, a fine grotto that was inside exactly like a house. When they had entered, the stag changed into an Ogre, and said to the boy: " Now you are my prisoner; you shall stop here and be my servant to the end of your days."

The next day the same thing happened to Cecchitiello, then to Nuccio, and so forth, until the seven brothers were all prisoners and servants of the Ogre, and the poor mother was in despair, not knowing what had happened to her handsome sons.

At the end of the month, however, a beautiful little girl was born to Cianna out of the myrtle tree, just as the old woman had prophesied, and Cianna called her Mortella, because out of a mortella (myrtle tree) she had been born.

Mortella was charming as well as pretty, a real help and comfort to her mother. Yet the seven boys could never be forgotten by the loving mother, who soon began telling Mortella how she had been born and how her brothers had disappeared after having found the water that had given her life. So little by little a great longing came to the child to go and find her brothers, and one fine evening, when all the stars shone in the dark blue sky, and Cianna and Mortella were sitting on

the balcony looking towards the wood, she begged her mother to let
her go and find her brothers.

At first Cianna would not hear of it. She was old, she said; she
had only this one daughter; she was not going to lose her and remain
all alone to spend her old age without anyone around her. But the
girl begged and prayed so much, and also the poor mother did so long
for news of her seven sons, that at last she allowed Mortella to go,
dressed like a pilgrim, and having been told to be very careful, and to
come back as soon as possible.

Mortella walked and walked and walked, and by the evening she
came to a small inn by the wood of Selvascura, and as there were many
people there, talking and eating, she asked whether any one of them
had ever heard what had become of her seven brothers.

" I think I know," said a feeble old woman, as aged as Father Time
himself, who sat in a dark corner sucking oranges. " I believe they
have become the servants of Narsete, the Ogre of Selvascura. It is
a very long way to go for those who do not know the way, and also you
must be careful not to come near Narsete, my child, for the Ogre
does not eat men, but he gobbles up all the women that come within
his reach."

Mortella, terribly frightened at the thought of an Ogre eating her
up bones and all, yet delighted at the news she had had of her brothers,
went cautiously to the wood the next day, and, after wandering some
time, she came within sight of the grotto and saw Gennariello cutting
wood. She knew him at once for her brother, because Cianna had
described them all carefully to her, so she went up to him and told him
who she was. Gennariello was amazed but delighted to see the sister
he and his brothers had longed so much for, and for whose sake they
had become the servants of the Ogre. He immediately took her to the
others, who were working indoors, for the Ogre was out hunting at the
time. They all rejoiced to see her, and taking her to their rooms told
her to keep very quiet with them for a while, and they would think of
some means of all getting out of Narsete's clutches.

Thus Mortella was shut up in her brothers' kitchen and told never
to go out of the room, to do all the work that there was to do, and

"MORTELLA WAS A REAL HELP AND COMFORT TO HER MOTHER."

never forget to share everything she ate with the cat, for it was a vicious cat that might do her harm.

Mortella did as she was told, and for a few days all went as well as possible; her brothers were greatly pleased to have her with them, and she was quite happy doing the housework and playing with the cat, waiting for the happy day when they all should go back home. One day Nuccio brought her a fine cake, and Mortella, who was rather greedy, ate it all without giving the cat its share; and the cat was so annoyed that it went and dropped a potful of water on the fire, putting it out. Poor Mortella did not know how to light it again, for she had no matches, and, forgetting her brothers' warning, she ran out of the room, went to the Ogre's kitchen, and took some burning coals out of the fire.

Narsete, who was not very far off, began to shout: "I smell a woman! Where is she? Let me have her roasted for my breakfast!"

Mortella, hearing this, ran madly to her room, locked it and piled all the furniture against the door; while Narsete, having sharpened his big knife, came rushing up and tried to pull down the door, which fortunately was very strong.

Hearing all this noise, the seven brothers came running in, and when they heard what it was all about they said to the Ogre: "We do not know how this wicked woman has managed to get into our room; but if you come with us, we'll show you a way of getting into the room without her noticing it, and you'll be able to kill her without the least trouble."

Saying this, they led Narsete to the back of the house, where they had dug a huge pit, and, pushing him from behind, they threw him right down to the bottom and then filled the pit with earth. So that was Narsete's end, and he could do no more harm.

After this the seven brothers and Mortella were owners of the Ogre's grotto and of all the riches it contained; but as the winter was very rough they decided to stop there until the good season, when they would take all the things back to their parents and live happily with them. "Do whatever you please and be the Queen of our home," said the seven brothers to Mortella; "but remember this: never on any account gather any grass or plant or flower grown on the place where

Narsete is buried, or the greatest harm will happen to us. Do not forget that through your disobeying us once you ran the greatest of risks, and be careful."

Moitella, still very much frightened at the thought of the Ogre running about the house with that sharpened knife in his hand trying to kill her, promised her brothers, whom she loved dearly, never to go near the place. So they lived happily together for the greater part of the winter, and as spring was approaching they began to think of the journey home, and of the pleasure their parents would have when they saw them all come back, safe and sound, and very rich into the bargain.

One day, as all the brothers were in the wood cutting timber to make carts to carry their things home, up came to the grotto a pilgrim who cried and wailed loudly, as he was in great pain. When he saw Mortella he told her that as he came to the wood he had seen a big wild-cat sitting on the branch of a pine tree, and as he stopped to look at it, the vicious

beast, feeling offended, had thrown a fir-cone at him with all its strength, hitting him in the neck, the result being a large hole which caused the poor man so much pain that he felt sure he was going to die.

"What can I do for you ? " asked Mortella kindly. " I'll do anything to get you out of your suffering."

"Only a poultice of rosemary can heal my wound," said the pilgrim, " but I do not think rosemary grows so far from the seaside."

"Wait a moment and I'll see if I can find any." Mortella ran out to look for rosemary, and saw a fine shrub of it growing right on the top of the Ogre's grave. In the joy of being able to bring the poor pilgrim some comfort, she forgot her brothers' warning and hastened

to gather the rosemary and make a poultice, which she put on the pilgrim's neck, and it immediately began to heal.

But, as she was getting the table ready for the midday meal, seven white doves flew on to the window-sill and said : " Oh, sister ours, why have you been so foolish ? Now for the sake of healing the pilgrim you have ruined all of us, your brothers, just at the time when we were about to take you home. We are going to be the easy prey of all the birds that haunt the forest, and in a few days we shall be eaten up by falcons, and hawks, and wildcats, unless you can get the Mother of Father Time to tell you what we must do to be turned once more into human beings."

On hearing this, Mortella began to weep as hard as she could; then she begged her brothers to stop in the house for fear that anything might harm them while she went to find Father Time's Mother.

" Mind you, it is very far, and we cannot even direct you," said the seven doves.

" Never mind that; I'll walk on and on, asking my way as I go. I'll provide you with plenty of food, so that you need not go out while I am away."

After having said good-bye to the seven beautiful white birds, which were all now sitting disconsolately in a row on the kitchen table, Mortella walked away as fast as she could, until she arrived at the seaside, and here, at a place where the waves were beating the shore with a mighty strength, caught between the rough sea and the cliff she saw a huge whale that was trying in vain to get out into the open water. When the whale saw Mortella, it cried: " Where are you going to, my pretty child ? "

" I am looking for the Mother of Father Time," answered Mortella; " could you tell me the way to her house ? "

" Go straight along the beach until you come to the place where the waves are so rough that they reach the highest point of the cliff. Then turn to the right and you'll find someone else to direct you. And, please, when you see the Mother of Father Time, ask her what I can do to get away to sea, for at present I cannot swim two yards without being thrown either on the shore or against the cliff."

" I shall certainly ask whatever you wish for, if I ever do get there. Good-bye, Whale."

On went Mortella along the fine grey sand, until she reached the spot where the waters beat the top of the cliff. Then she turned to the right, and hardly had she gone ten yards through the beautiful country-side, full of lovely flowers, when a mouse came up to her and said :

" Where are you off to, my pretty girl ? "

" I am going to the house of Father Time's Mother, pretty Mouse," answered Mortella; " have you any idea where it may be ? "

" It is a long way off," sighed the Mouse, " yet do not be discouraged, for you'll arrive there in time if you persevere. You go straight
on through those beautiful fields until you get to the foot of that
mountain ; there somebody else will show you the way."

" Thank you, Mouse, and can I do anything for you ? "

" Yes, you can," said the Mouse eagerly ; " when you get there,
please ask the old woman what we mice can do to get out of the power
of the cat. I am the King of Mouseland, and if you can get us that
precious information, both myself and my subjects will be at your orders
now and evermore."

" I will certainly, dear little King Mouse ; and now good-bye and
many thanks."

" Good-bye, Mortella, and good luck to you ! "

The mountains from that place seemed quite near, but that is an
old trick mountains have on very fine days. As Mortella went on they
seemed to get further away, yet she tried to be brave and not grow
discouraged, and eventually she came to where she longed to be. As
she arrived she saw on the ground a lengthy procession of ants who were
carrying home a quantity of wheat.

" Where are you going to all alone, my beautiful one ? " asked
the largest ant, who was carrying a seed far bigger than herself.

" I am looking for the house of Father Time's Mother," replied
Mortella.

" Go through that narrow passage between the mountains, and when
you get to the plain, walk straight in front of you ; there you'll find someone to direct you. Cheer up ! you have not to go very far now."

" Thank you, kind Ant. Can I do anything for you ? "

" Yes, please ask the Mother of Father Time what we ants can do
to have a longer life, for it seems useless to work so hard and get so
many riches and hoard so much wheat in our granaries when we die
as soon as our work is done, so that we never have the enjoyment of
what we work for."

" I certainly will. Good-bye, Ant."

By the evening of the next day Mortella had crossed the plain
and had come to a place where a beautiful oak several centuries old

"SEVEN WHITE DOVES FLEW ON TO THE WINDOW-SILL."

was throwing its shadow on the field.   When the old tree saw the young
girl, he called out to her :

"Come and rest awhile under my shade, you look so tired."

"Thank you, kind Oak," replied Mortella; "that I would with the
greatest pleasure, but I am seeking the house of the Mother of Father
Time, and must lose no moment in finding it."

"You are not very far from it now, and if you go on quickly enough
you'll be there before to-night.   But if you do get there, please ask
the old woman what I can do to get my honour back.   I used to be
the pride of this land, and now I am reduced to feeding the pigs
with my acorns."

"I certainly will.   Good-bye, Oak."

Off ran Mortella, wild with joy at the idea of being so near her
goal, thinking of her brothers who were at home waiting for her, and of
her joy when she should see them once more.

As the Oak had said, by the end of the afternoon she came to the
foot of a rather steep hill, on the top of which was the long-sought-for
house.   As Mortella, drooping with fatigue, sat down on a stone to
rest awhile and recover her breath, she saw lying on a heap of hay
close by an old man almost bent double, and she knew him at once for
the old pilgrim who had been the innocent cause of all her troubles.

He looked up and immediately recognised her, and exclaimed :

"How sorry I am, my daughter, for all this trouble you are going
through!   I am no good to anybody now, and I shall soon be no more,
but before I die I will give you some good advice, so that I can do you
a little good, for all you have done for me.

"When you have climbed to the top of that hill, you will find an
old house, so old that it looks as if the walls were going to tumble to
ruins at any minute; everything is dusty and covered with spider webs.
After you have gone through the rusty gates, you'll see some broken
pillars, and, sitting on them, a snake biting its tongue, a stag and a
raven and a phœnix.   Take no notice of these, but go straight in;
you will then see all round the walls little heaps of ashes, each bearing
the name of a famous city of the days gone by.   In this room you must
hide yourself behind the great timepiece, and wait there for Father

"FATHER TIME WENT FLYING OUT."
From "The Child of the Myrtle Tree"

Time to go out. When you are sure he is quite out of hearing, go straight into the other room, and there you will find an old woman sitting on a clock, her hair all wound up round about her, like an enormous horse's tail, a long scraggy beard that touches the floor, and a face so wrinkled that it is impossible to distinguish any features. The first thing for you to do as you enter must be to take off the weights of the clock, so that the clock will stop and the old woman will be obliged to give you whatever you ask for. But if she swears by anything you must be very careful that she swears by her son's wings, because if she swears by anything else she will not keep her promise. Now good-bye, and may you be very lucky in this last part of your journey."

Greatly comforted by these kind words, Mortella wended her way up the hill and found everything exactly as the old pilgrim had said. As she came to the room where the ashes of the ancient cities were kept, she hid behind the timepiece just as Father Time went flying out. He was a hugely tall old man with long white hair falling down to his feet, and a thick and long white beard, a large scythe in his right hand, and a pair of scales in the left; on his back was a pair of enormous white wings that swept the room as he came through and flew with a great noise out of the window. No sooner had he gone than Mortella, who could see him no instant longer—for he flew away so fast that in less than a second he had gone a thousand miles,—went into the next room, where Father Time's Mother was sitting on the clock, and quickly she took off the weights, and then asked the old woman for what she wished. Father Time's Mother immediately called out to her son, but Mortella stopped her quickly by saying:

" It is of no use your calling your son, for I have taken the weights and he cannot move until I put them back."

Then the old woman began to beg and pray:

" Please, darling, put them back, and I will give you whatever you wish for, I promise you."

" No, I won't," said Mortella.

" Give me back the weights, and I swear by my son's head that you shall get whatever you wish for."

" No."

" Give them back to me, and I swear by my son's hands and feet that you'll get your wish."

And yet Mortella would not give them back until the old woman saw that there was no getting out of it, and said :

" Very well, then, if you put them back, I swear by my son's wings, that fly everywhere, that I'll tell you whatever you wish to know."

Then Mortella put the weights back and kissed the old woman's wrinkled hand. This act of courtesy greatly touched the old lady, who said kindly :

" You go and hide behind that door, and when my son comes in I'll get him to say whatever you want ; but don't let him see you, for he is most unforgiving even with his own children, and would eat you up without leaving you time to say : ' Oh ! ' "

As soon as Mortella had told Father Time's Mother what she wished to know, she hid behind the door, and when her son returned his mother began asking him many questions, begging him to answer her. And Father Time, after being prayed and besought a long while, finally said :

" Tell the tree that he will be loved again by all men when he has got rid of the treasure hidden under his roots. The mice shall be freed from the cat when they have tied a bell to its tail, so that they can hear it come. The ants shall live a hundred years if they stop growing wings, for when an ant begins to fly, it means that it is going to die. If the whale will make friends with the sea-serpent, he will take her safely and surely through the hidden ways of the deep sea. As to the seven doves, they shall be turned once more into men when they rest on the columns of riches."

Having said this, Father Time flew once more out of the window, and Mortella, having thanked the old woman, ran to the foot of the hill, where she found the seven doves, which had followed her in her travels. As they were tired after having flown so far, they all sat down on the horns of a dead ox that had been left in the field, to listen to their sister's tale, and suddenly they were all turned into young men.

Because the horn is the symbol of riches, and thus the oracle spoken by Father Time had been accomplished.

As they came to the Oak, they stopped and told it what Father Time had said : then the Oak begged them to take away the treasure and keep in for their trouble, and the young men, having found a spade, began digging until they found a big sack full of gold. The Oak was very much pleased, and they parted the best of friends.

As the evening drew near, being all very tired, they lay down under a walnut tree and fell asleep. But as they slept, a band of thieves came and tied them up with strong ropes, and took the gold and fled.

" Ah ! woe is us ! " cried the poor things. " Now not only have

we lost our gold, but nothing else is left to us except to die of hunger or be eaten by a wolf."

As they were crying thus, the King Mouse came round, and Mortella told him that Father Time had said they must tie a bell to the cat's tail to avoid being caught. The King Mouse was so pleased with the good advice that he whistled sharply, and suddenly hundreds and thousands of

mice came up from Mouseland, and they began gnawing at the ropes until sister and brothers were all set free and able to go on their way again.

After a while they met the Ants and stopped to tell them what they must do to live a hundred years.

" Why so sad ? " inquired the big Ant gratefully. " If there is anything we can do for you, that we will, for you have done us a very good turn."

" The thieves have robbed us of our treasure, and there is no hope of our ever getting it back."

" Why no hope ? Of course I know who has taken your treasure. It is the thieves of Musariello, and they hide their treasures under a heap of dried leaves in a log cabin not far from here. I'll lead you there if you come with me. I saw them hiding a big sack last night, and they won't be there, for I heard them say they were going to Naples to-day."

The young people followed the Ant, and, as she had said, they found their treasure hidden in the log cabin under the dried leaves. Then, having thanked the kind little creature, they hurried on their way to the sea, wondering how they could ever get back to Amalfi and to their dear parents.

As they were sitting on the shore, the Whale came up, and Mortella told her how she could make her way to the deep by becoming friends with the Sea-Serpent. At that very moment Gennariello uttered a cry of terror. He had seen the thieves running in their direction with knives in their hands. When the Whale saw them in this new trouble she said :

" Your sister has been so kind to me, and I want to help you. Jump quickly on my back and I'll take you safely home."

They all jumped, and in the greatest hurry, for the thieves were getting dangerously near, and off went the Whale, at the rate of twenty miles an hour, leaving the thieves storming on the beach.

When they had travelled for one day and one night, the Whale put them all safely down on the shore at Amalfi, and swam off to look for the Sea-Serpent, without waiting to be thanked.

The young people ran back to their home and found their parents seated by the window, waiting for them to return. How happy they were to see them all, looking bright and healthy, and so kind and loving towards each other !

Later on they went and fetched all the great riches that had been left by Narsete, and the family lived happily together for ever after, in a fine house by the sea, remembering that a good deed is never lost, and that a kind action is worth all the riches of the world.

FILADORO

IN the days of long ago there was, not far from Naples, a beautiful wood of fig-trees and poplars, so tall and thick that the rays of the sun could not get through the dark green foliage. In the very thickest part of this wood stood a tiny cottage, made of stones heaped up as luck would have it, and all tumbling to ruins because for years and years nobody had ever repaired it. The furniture consisted of one plank supported by four bricks, which stood for a table, a log that was meant for a chair, and a heap of straw which served as a bed.

In this miserable place there lived an old woman, so old that the birds of the forest always remembered having seen her just as she was now; so ugly and wrinkled and bent that, whenever she went anywhere near the houses of the neighbouring villages, the children ran away frightened, shouting : " Here comes the Witch of Boscofatato ! Get away ! Get away ! "

This unfortunate old woman was so poor that very often she had nothing but roots to eat, for the wood was thick and nothing would grow under it ; and when the figs were not ripe she lived on alms, and they were not often given her.

One day when she had been obliged to fast for nearly a week, after a long walk in search of food, she found an old man who gave her an apronful of beans. Beaming with joy at the thought of the fine dinner she was going to enjoy, she went back home as fast as her old legs would allow her, carrying the beans as if they had been something holy, and, having put the precious things with loving care into the best of her two pots (it was an earthenware pot, with only one handle and all cracked), she placed it on the window-sill to keep fresh, and then went into the wood to look for some dead branches with which to light the fire.

As her bad luck would have it, who should come into the wood of Boscofatato that day but the son of the King of Naples, who had taken it into his head that he wanted to enjoy himself far from the Court and do what he pleased. No sooner had Nard' Aniello—for such was the Prince's name—seen the old cottage and the potful of beans on the window-sill than the idea entered his thoughtless head that it would be the greatest fun to take shots at it to see which of them all (he had some followers with him) could hit it right in the middle.

So they began throwing stones, and, just as the old woman was returning with a small faggot of wood in her apron, Nard' Aniello caught the middle of the pot with a big stone, smashed it to pieces, and sent the beans scattering about in the mud.

When the poor old dame saw her long-sought and much-wished-for dinner wasted on the ground, and the pot broken, she flew, as you can easily imagine, into a red-hot fury, and shouting at the Prince with all her might, she said : " May you fall into the hands of an Ogress and be treated by her, not like a Prince, but like the least of the servants ; may you fall in love with the daughter, so that you are tormented for the sake of the daughter ; and may you in the end be boiled alive

and eaten by the ugliest Ogress in the world!"

Nard' Aniello merely laughed at this terrible malediction, because he did not believe in old women casting spells; and on he went through the wood, leaving his companions scattered about in various directions.

Suddenly he stopped and gazed in rapture. Under the shade of a beautiful thick poplar, a lovely girl was sitting on the cool green grass, and in front of her, crawling on the sward, was a long procession of snails, with handsome bright shells, and she was calling to them, saying:

> "Oh, little snail, put out your horn!
> Your mother is calling you home
> To see your brother who has just been born."

And all the snails came up to her, and she took them up gently in her hands, and fed them with special leaves that snails are very fond of. Nard' Aniello had seen many beautiful girls in his life; but none that he had seen so far had that luxuriant hair rippling in thick curls almost to her feet, those dark eyes, shining like stars, such a complexion of lilies and roses, and such tiny white hands, so gentle and pretty. As he stood there gazing in wonder and admiration, the girl looked up, and as the Prince fell in love with her, so she fell in love with the Prince, for indeed he was a very handsome youth, and possessed the pleasantest smile and the most brilliant and merry eyes in the world.

For a little while they stood gazing at each other, then Nard' Aniello seemed all at once to recover his voice and said :

"Oh, the prettiest of all fairy visions! How is it that you are lost in this wood where nobody can see you? Why should the towns be deprived of such a beauty? Give me your hand to kiss, fair one: I love you most desperately!"

At these words Filadoro blushed, looking a thousand times prettier, and gave the Prince her hand for him to kiss, with a manner that would not have disgraced a queen. But just as the enraptured Prince was raising it to his lips, a shower of angry words fell upon him.

It was the fearful Ogress, mother of Filadoro, a wicked, ugly Ogress that lived in the woodland and was always on the look-out for some young fresh meat to eat: how she could ever have had such a gem as Filadoro for her daughter was a mystery that none could ever understand. Now, after she had sworn at the Prince, she beat him with a stick and pushed him towards her house, saying : "If by to-night you have not dug this five-acre field and sown this wheat, I shall flay you alive and eat you!"

After this, she went to have a chat with the other Ogresses of the wood, and told them of the good luck that had sent her a Prince to eat. How tender and fresh his flesh would be!

Meanwhile poor Nard' Aniello was sitting on a log, looking desolately at the field he was to dig. How could he possibly attempt to do it? He had never held a spade in his hand in all his life! And as he thought that the Ogress would flay him alive and eat him, his eyes filled with tears. Never again would he see his mother, and his kingdom, and the beautiful sea that stretched for miles in front of his marble palace. . . .

As he was thus musing on the sad fate his naughty doings of the morning had brought upon his miserable head, a gentle hand was laid upon his shoulder and Filadoro's sweet voice said gently : "Why so sad? Are you not pleased that we are here together and that we love each other so?" "What is the good?" replied Nard' Aniello sadly, "if I am going to be eaten by your mother to-night? It is impossible for me to dig and sow the field before she comes back." " Don't you worry about such trifles, my own love," said Filadoro caressingly ; " the field shall be dug and sown before my mother comes back. Now come and let us be happy together."

In the evening, as the first stars began to peep out on the still clear sky, the Prince rushed to the field, and when the Ogress came back she found him standing, a spade on his shoulder, an empty wheat-sack by him, and a well-dug and well-sown field before him.

This of course very much surprised the old woman, yet she said nothing, and sent the Prince to sleep in the pig-sty. The following morning she came out on to the balcony and showed Nard' Aniello the trunks of four big oaks, saying : " By to-night all these must be cut up so that they can be put into the kitchen stove. If it is not done properly, I shall cut you into small pieces and make a fine stew of you."

Having said this, she called out to Filadoro to put down her hair, and off she went to gossip with the other Ogresses. There was no staircase in the house, and Filadoro had to put down her hair for her mother to get up and down.

After the Ogress had gone, Nard' Aniello stood musing before the wood he had to cut. Of course he could not even attempt to do it. For one thing, he was a Prince and not a wood-cutter : he had never seen an axe before. Secondly, it would have taken not one but three wood-cutters to do all that work in such a short time. There was nothing to be done but to make a good stew for the Ogress's dinner.

But at this moment came Filadoro, climbing down by her own hair, which she had tied on to the balcony, and again she told him not to worry, but to come with her, and that the tree trunks would take care of themselves. By the evening, wonderful to relate, all the wood was cut, and the Ogress could not find fault with the Prince.

The next morning she ordered him to empty a huge tank about the size of a big lake, and went off muttering that she would eat him all the same in the evening, for she liked fresh meat, and she felt sure there was somebody helping him.

Filadoro came down looking very much worried.

" We must get away this moment," she said in a distressed tone,

"SUDDENLY HE STOPPED AND GAZED IN RAPTURE."
From "Filadoro."

"for I fear my mother has found out I am helping you, and she will kill us both if she knows it for certain. Also she is determined to eat you to-night."

"Oh, my darling!" exclaimed Nard' Aniello, "if only you could get me out of the clutches of this horrid creature, I would take you to Naples and marry you the

moment we arrive. But how can we go without the Ogress knowing about it?"

Filadoro then ran up to the house, and, taking a big potful of macaroni she had been getting ready for dinner, she gave a spoonful of it to everything inside the house, so that they should keep silent about her going away. In the Ogress's house all things were magic, and if something went wrong they cried out so that the Ogress could rush home and see to it. Then off she went with Nard' Aniello, and they ran as fast as ever they could until they came to Pozzuli. Once there and out of danger the Prince said : "My lovely bride, it is not fair that I should take you to the palace badly dressed as you are. Wait for me in this inn, and I will come and fetch you with a beautiful dress and a carriage and all my Court, so that you shall enter Naples as my Queen."

Filadoro was very much pleased at this, and said that she would wait.
But in the morning, in her hurry to get away, she had forgotten to give
a spoonful of macaroni to her looking-glass, which in consequence was
very cross. As it rather loved Filadoro it kept silent until the evening;
but when the Ogress had come home and she began asking every piece
of furniture where her daughter and the prisoner had gone to, it could
not resist saying that they had gone together to Naples, where they
hoped to get married.

" That they never shall," shouted the infuriated Ogress. " May
Nard' Aniello forget her the moment he is kissed by another woman ! "

Just as she was saying this the Prince was entering the palace, and
the Queen his mother, mad with joy—for she had so feared he had
been killed in some accident,—ran up to him and, throwing her arms
round his neck, she kissed him. And, because of the Ogress's malediction, the Prince forgot at once all about Filadoro.

Meanwhile the poor girl was waiting and waiting in the inn at
Pozzuli, but wait as she would, the days went by and her lover never
returned. Filadoro felt bitterly disappointed, because she could not
possibly go back to her mother ; also, she was so fond of Nard' Aniello
that she would have given anything to be with him. Neither could
she understand what had happened to him, for she knew he loved her
and that he would never have forsaken her.

As she was crying, looking out of the window to see if he came,
a little white dove flew on to her shoulder. It was Filadoro's pet
dove, which she had saved from the clutches of a hawk. The girl was
greatly pleased to see her pet, and began stroking it tenderly. Then
the dove told her of the Ogress's malediction, also that the Prince was
about to marry a wicked Princess of the neighbouring kingdom that
very day. When Filadoro heard this she immediately told the dove
to fly to the palace and tell the servants to come to the inn, for she
had a present for the Prince and his bride. The servants came, and
Filadoro, taking a sharp knife, tore her beautiful white arm open, pulled
out a marvellous scarf made of gold and fine gems, and gave it to the
servants, saying : " This is my wedding present for the Princess."

The amazed servants ran back to the palace, and brought the

"EVERYBODY WAS LONGING TO TASTE IT."

scarf to the bride, who was sitting in the throne room with Nard'
Aniello, and they told her how the beautiful lady had got it. When
the bride, who was as envious as a cat, heard of this she said : " Oh,
but that is nothing : I can do much better myself," and she ordered a
sharp knife to be brought to her. But as she tore her arm open she
fell to the floor and died.

A little later Nard' Aniello was forced to take another bride, the
sister of the envious Princess. Again Filadoro sent for his servants :
she was not living in the inn now, but had taken a small house in which
everything was charmed, and where all the work was done by the
pieces of furniture. So when the servants rang at the door it opened
by itself, and a magic staircase took them up to Filadoro's room. There
the girl had a frying-pan full of boiling oil brought to her—as a matter
of fact, she merely clapped her hands and the pan came rushing along
—and she shook her hand in it, producing some beautiful golden fishes
which she gave to the servants on a gold plate, ordering them to present
them to the bride. Again the servants told how these things had
happened ; and the bride, on hearing it, at once said : " Oh, I can do
much better ! " and she had some boiling oil brought to her. But when
she put her fingers into it she scalded herself so badly that she died.

Nard' Aniello was getting rather annoyed at the way his brides
had to die for their stupid envy. Yet, to please the Queen his mother,
he consented to marry the last of the sisters, who was as bad as the
others, if not worse. This time Filadoro entered a red-hot oven and
came out with a marvellous cake. No one had ever seen the like in
the whole of the kingdom of Naples, so beautiful it was, all decorated
with flowers and crystallised fruits of every kind. It smelt so delicious,
too, that everybody was longing to taste it, and when they had tasted it
they declared that no such cake had ever before been made upon earth.

When the bride heard how it had been made, she immediately
said she knew how to do the same, if not better. Nard' Aniello tried to
persuade her to let things alone, and not come to her sisters' bad end.
But she insisted so much that at last Nard' Aniello grew very angry and
said that she might die for all he cared. So she entered the red-hot
oven and of course made no cake and was burnt to death.

Then the Prince determined that he would go and see who it was that, innocently or otherwise, had caused his three brides to die, and he was taken by the servants to Filadoro's fairy house. As Nard' Aniello came in sight, the doors opened by themselves and the bells rang out: " Welcome, beautiful Prince ! " Nard' Aniello was very much surprised. But as he was taken upstairs, there was Filadoro, as lovely as she was when he had first seen her in the wood, her golden tresses longer and brighter than ever, her complexion like lilies and roses, her beautiful dark eyes full of loving light. And as soon as their eyes met the spell was broken, and the Prince took her into his arms and brought her back to Naples, in the greatest hurry for fear the Ogress might once more come between them and do them harm.

Then Nard' Aniello told his parents about all his adventures in the wood of Boscofatato, and how Filadoro had saved his life.

So there was one of the grandest weddings that ever was, and the Prince and Filadoro lived happy for ever after in the splendid marble palace by the deep blue sea. And the Prince never again caused harm to poor people, for he had learnt the lesson that it is very wicked to give trouble and pain to others simply to amuse oneself. He was so good that all his subjects loved him, and only spoke of him as " The good Prince with the Fairy Bride."

7

THE FAIRY KITTENS

ONCE, long ago, there lived in Southern Italy a woman called Caradonia. She had a tiny cottage on a hillside planted with olive-trees and cactuses, and covered with grass that in summer-time was burnt as brown as it could be by the hot sun. There she lived with her two daughters, Cecella and Grandizia.

That is to say, Grandizia was Caradonia's own child, and she was a spoilt little thing, as ugly as ugly can be, with a sallow complexion, unkempt hair, and a squint; besides that, she was the rudest, most disagreeable little being that ever came to walk on this earth. Cecella, on the contrary, was a sweetly pretty girl, obliging and obedient, always ready to do things for everybody in need ; but, as she was Caradonia's step-daughter, she was hated both by her and by Grandizia, who made her do all the roughest work in the house and let her go about dressed in rags, whilst Grandizia sat all the morning on the balcony, dressed in a fine costume, playing about with her spinning-wheel. Yet in spite of all this everybody who came near Cecella admired her and loved her, while Grandizia was disliked by everybody, not because she was plain, for that was not her fault, but because she was so terribly rude and disobliging.

Both the mother and the daughter were always trying some way of finding fault with Cecella, to have a pretext for beating her, and one morning Cecella, after having done all the house-work (while Grandizia sat at the looking-glass trying to make herself look beautiful, which she never did), was sent out with the goat and given a pound of tow to spin. That was far too much for the little girl to do, so that, when the evening came and she returned home, in spite of having worked the whole day without stopping, only half of the tow was spun. Caradonia was very cross, and, taking a stick, she cruelly beat poor little Cecella, and sent her to bed supperless.

The next morning, as Cecella went out with the goat, her step-mother gave her two pounds of tow to spin, saying in the harshest way that if it was not spun by evening she would be beaten even worse than on the previous day, and would have to go without meals for a whole day.

The little girl went her way disconsolately, dragging the goat behind her by the lead and holding the tow under her arm, looking altogether a picture of misery. When she came to the field where the goat was wont to graze, she threw herself on the bank of a brooklet that meandered cheerily through the meadow, and began to sob her little heart out.

At that moment a wrinkled, crippled little old woman came by, struggling to carry a faggot of wood that was far too heavy for her ; and as Cecella looked up and saw this she forgot all her own troubles and ran up to the woman, asking very politely : " Please, madam, may I help you with your faggot ? "

"Thank you, my child," answered the woman, "I should be very much obliged to you if you would, for I am getting old and weak." So Cecella, who was very strong for her age, took the faggot on her own shoulders, and carried it to a little cottage not far from the brook. As she put it down the old woman said in a kind tone:

"I believe you were crying when I met you: tell me what is your trouble?"

"My mother has given me two pounds of tow to spin," sobbed out Cecella, "and if it is not all finished by to-night she is going to beat me. And I can't do it: I tried hard to do one pound yesterday, and could not!"

"Is that all the trouble? Well, I'll teach you a way out of it, because you are such a good, kind little girl. Stroke your goat gently on the back and say:

'Kiddie, Kiddie, spin my tow,
And you'll be fed with the grass I mow.'

As you say this, put the tow by the goat, and then go and mow some nice grass and take it to her. All will be right then."

Cecella, as pleased as pleased could be, went cheerily back to the field and did exactly as the old woman had told her, so that when she came back home all the tow was spun, to Caradonia's great surprise and disappointment.

The next day the wicked step-mother gave Cecella four pounds of tow to spin, because she felt sure it would be impossible for the girl to tackle all that in the day. Yet, as she felt there was some mystery about the spinning of the previous day, she ordered Grandizia to follow Cecella, and see who helped her to spin. Grandizia went out on tiptoe, and when she came to the field she hid herself behind a thick Indian fig-bush, in the wood by the brooklet. From that hiding-place she saw Cecella giving the goat the tow to spin while she gathered some fresh grass for the animal to eat, and Grandizia ran back home to tell her mother. They were both so annoyed that when Cecella came home they killed the goat and ate it for dinner, giving Cecella only the bones. After supper, Cecella as usual went to the kitchen to do the washing-up, and took up the bones to throw them in the dustbin. But just as she was about to do so, a voice whispered into her ear: " Do not throw the bones away, but take them all carefully and bury them in the garden." Cecella, obedient as usual, did as she was told, and after that she went to bed.

As soon as she was out of hearing, Caradonia said to Grandizia : " I have such a good idea ! Let us send Cecella to the fairies to ask them for a sieve. They are so horrid, as everybody knows, that they are sure to scratch her badly, and then she will be pretty no more."

Grandizia was exceedingly pleased at this, and early next morning Cecella was called and ordered to go to the fairies. The girl, who had heard that the fairies of Grottapelata were very wicked, felt rather frightened and begged not to be sent ; but Caradonia threatened to beat her if she did not go at once and come back with the sieve ; so, of course, she went, and wended her way through the wood with tears filling her big blue eyes.

Now, as she was walking she suddenly met her friend, the old

woman, who came up to her and
stroked her hair, saying : " Why, crying again ? What is the matter now ? "
" I must go to the fairies of
Grottapelata to borrow a
sieve, and I am afraid to
go, because I am told they
are so cruel."

" Listen to me, dearie :
when you reach the palace,
you will be asked to put
a finger in the keyhole :
don't you do it, but put a
small stick instead. For
the rest, I trust you to
follow your kind nature
and do the best you can
to make yourself pleasant
to everybody. Now,
good-bye and good luck
to you, my child ! "

Having said this, the old woman disappeared through an Indian
fig-tree, and Cecella went on her way, feeling very much cheered.
Before long she arrived at the palace door and knocked, and a voice
from inside cried : " Put your finger into the keyhole." Cecella put in
a small stick she had picked up in the wood. The stick was broken, the
door opened, and the fairies, who were all sitting together in the hall
working on magic spells, told her to look round the house, while they
finished what they were doing. They would then get the sieve ready.

First of all Cecella arrived at a very large room, and found it
absolutely full of all manner of kittens—black, white, blue, tawny,
tiger-marked,—one prettier than the other. One was dusting, another
sewing, another trying to light the fire, another cooking ; some were
washing up ; all were working hard, and went about on their little hind
legs looking very busy.

"THINK OF THEM DOING ALL THAT ROUGH WORK!"

" Oh, the darlings ! " cried out Cecella, leaping with excitement.
" Are they not pretty ?   Think of them doing all that rough work with
those dear little paws !   I'll do it ! " and she set to work hard herself.
She was so used to house-work that she was very good at it, and presently the room was dusted and swept, the fire lit, the plates washed up
and dried, the sewing done, everything tidily put away ; then she sat
down on a chair, a kitten on each shoulder, one on her knee, and all the
others dancing about her merrily.   At this moment an enormous black
cat, as dark as a starless night, called Gatto Mammone, came into the
room, and all the kittens took each other by the paw and danced in circle,
singing :   " Miaou, miaou, miaou !   Cecella has done all our work ! "

Gatto Mammone was very much pleased, and asked : " What will
you have for lunch ?   Bread and onion, or cake ? "

" Bread and onion," replied Cecella.   " That is what I am used to."

" And cake and fruit you shall have," said Gatto Mammone, getting
it ready for her.

After Cecella had her lunch, Gatto Mammone took her up a lovely
glass staircase ; but, before going up, the girl took off her clogs, and
walked very lightly on tip-toe, so that she should not break the steps.
On the second floor Gatto Mammone led Cecella into a beautiful
room, where there were spread on some tables silk and cotton dresses,
gold, silver, and copper coins, diamond and bead earrings, and told
her to choose what she wished.   Cecella took a cotton dress, a handful
of copper coins, and a pair of bead earrings.   Gatto Mammone was
much pleased to see how modest she was, and he gave her a beautiful
silk costume, a bag full of gold, and a pair of diamond earrings.   Then
he said : " As you go out of the gate, you will hear an ass braying, but
don't turn round.   But when you hear the cock crowing, look up."

Cecella, as pleased and happy as a little girl could be—nobody had
ever been so kind to her in all her life, and she had never seen anything
so beautiful as the cat's presents,—made a fine curtsey, said good-bye to
the kittens, and, having taken up the sieve that was ready in the hall, set
forth homewards.   As she went an ass brayed loudly : " Ih-ah, ih-ah ! "
but Cecella took no notice.   Then a cock crowed : " Cock-a-doodle-do ! "
and immediately she looked up, and a lovely star fell on her forehead.

"THE FRUIT FELL BY ITSELF INTO THE BASKET."
From "The Fairy Kittens."

When Caradonia and Grandizia saw the girl come back unhurt and looking prettier than ever in the lovely clothes, they nearly fainted with rage, and they tried to take off the clothes and snatch the star away. But these were fairy garments, and could not be touched by anyone but those to whom they had been given.

When they had done with the sieve, Grandizia said : " I will take it back : there is no reason why I should not have even prettier garments than Cecella."

On her way she met the old woman, who said : " Where are you going to, my little girl ? "

" Get off and hold your tongue, you silly old thing ! " cried Grandizia in her disagreeable, croaky voice. " I go where I please."

" All right, all right, my pretty ; you go where you please."

When Grandizia came to the door, she was asked to put her finger into the keyhole, which she did. And her finger was pulled very badly and broken, so that when she got in she was so angry that she threw the sieve at the fairies, saying nasty words ; then she saw the kittens at work, and she pulled their ears and tails, kicked them about, and hurt them in every way, and the poor little things began to cry, and Gatto Mammone came in and was very angry with the cruel girl.

All the same he asked : " Will you have some bread and onion for lunch ? "

" Bread and onion ? How dare you offer me bread and onion ! You may eat that yourself : as for me, I'll only have cake, and of the best."

" And cake you shall have," answered Gatto Mammone, ordering one of the kittens to bring round some cake. But as soon as Grandizia had put it to her mouth it began to burn her and gave her a nasty pain, for it was a fairy cake, and bad people were hurt when they ate of it.

Then Gatto Mammone took her up the glass staircase, warning her to be careful ; but Grandizia ran up, weighing heavily on the glass with her clog-shod feet, and all the glass was smashed, which made Gatto Mammone very cross, while Grandizia was hurt by the sharp fragments. Presently they came to the room where all the dresses were

on exhibition, and immediately Grandizia chose the best silk frock,
a bag of gold, and a pair of diamond earrings ; but as she put them on
the dress turned to dirty rags, the gold was changed into dead leaves,
and the earrings into scorpions that hung to her ears by their pincers.
Grandizia at this felt angrier than ever, and she would have killed Gatto
Mammone ; but he was a wizard, and as Grandizia tried to get at him
he began to grow, and he grew and grew until he reached the ceiling and
disappeared through it.

Now, as Grandizia went out of the gate, the ass began to bray
loudly, and the girl turned round and shouted at him. At that very
moment an ass's tail fell on her forehead and stuck there. If she was
plain before, now, with that hideous thing hanging in front of her,

she was a dreadful
sight, and Cara-
donia was almost
beside herself with
rage and grief when
she saw her dar-
ling come home in
that condition.

A few days after
all this had hap-
pened the King
passed by on horse-
back, and, stopping
his horse before the
cottage door, said
to Caradonia :
" Please give me a
basketful of pome-
granates."

" That I would
be only too hon-
oured to do, your
Majesty," replied

Caradonia, " but in this part of the country there are no pomegranates, only Indian figs and olives."

" What do you mean by talking like that ? What about that fine tree growing at your very door ? " retorted the King angrily. Then Caradonia came out, and lo ! there was a wonderful tree grown all of a sudden by the cottage door, and in the dark foliage one could see the pretty red fruits all ripe and ready to be eaten. Caradonia was absolutely amazed, yet she apologised somehow or other and tried to gather a basketful of the beautiful fruit, but as she endeavoured to reach the lower branches they leapt up out of her reach.

" Is there no one in the place able to gather me some of this fruit ? " cried the King.

" My daughter may be able to, your Majesty," said Caradonia, calling out to Grandizia, who in the meanwhile had been sitting in front of her looking-glass trying to hide the ass's tail and painting her face in order to look prettier ; but all the white and pink paint, instead of improving her looks, made her appear even worse than before, if that were possible. Grandizia tried her best to gather the fruit, and even climbed up a ladder, but the branches kept on getting out of reach, and all her efforts were in vain.

" Have you no one else in the house ? " growled the King, who by now was quite angry.

" Oh yes, there is a kind of servant. But she is a little good-for-nothing, and she would not be able to do anything."

" Call her at once," commanded the King.

Caradonia could no longer refuse to obey his Majesty's orders, so she called out to Cecella to come down, and the girl came dressed in the fine dress the fairies had given her, the star on her forehead shining more brightly than ever ; and she was so beautiful, so like a fairy princess, that the King stared at her in rapt admiration.

Cecella curtseyed to the King with a grace that would have done honour to a court lady, and then went to the tree. The branches immediately lowered and the fruit fell by itself into the basket Cecella was holding. Of course, it was Cecella's own tree, sprung up from the bones of the little goat.

The King was so pleased with Cecella's beauty and her fine manners that he decided to marry her, and said that he would come on the morrow to fetch her.

Caradonia could not make any objections, of course ; but she begged the King to have the carriage in which Cecella was to travel made of iron, as the girl was far too delicate to travel in a glass carriage (the King always travelled in a glass carriage, so that all his subjects could look at him).

That night, while Cecella slept peacefully, dreaming of the happy life that was awaiting her, Caradonia went to the wood and hid Grandizia there under a cask.

Early in the morning the King came up with all his court and the iron carriage in which the bride was to travel. Cecella was dressed in her bridal dress, with a lovely veil and orange blossom that smelt so sweetly that the air all around was perfumed by it. Then she was made to sit in the carriage with Caradonia, while the King rode in front, and they began their journey towards the city of Dolabella.

As they reached the place where Grandizia was hiding, Caradonia asked for the carriage to stop, as Cecella wished to gather some rare flowers growing in that part of the wood. And she led the poor child into the depth of the forest, where Grandizia was waiting in the cask for them.

Poor little bride ! The two wicked women stripped her of all her beautiful clothes, gagged her and bound her hands and feet, and then put her under the cask, shutting it so that poor Cecella could hardly breathe. Then Caradonia dressed up Grandizia in the bridal dress, cut the ass's tail from her forehead, and over her face put a very thick white veil. When all this was done, they went running back to the carriage, which, as I have told you, was made of iron, so that from outside one could not see who was in it, and the royal train went on towards Dolabella, where his Majesty had his palace.

The King rode his fine white steed, spurring it on, for he was very anxious to get home and have his lovely bride all to himself : now and again he looked behind at the carriage that contained all he loved best in the world, even more than his own kingdom. Suddenly he noticed that the carriage was entirely surrounded by a whole army of kittens of all kinds and colours and sizes, and they mewed one more loudly than the other. These strange little kittens looked so pretty that nobody had the heart to

send them away ; yet it seemed so extraordinary that they should be there.   But as he listened to their mewing the King heard them saying :

"Miaou, miaou, miaou !
The pretty bride is in the cask,
The ugly one put on the mask.
Beautiful King, go back to the wood,
Take you your bride and give her some food."

The King was so surprised to hear kittens talk that he immediately went to the carriage and opened it ; and there were Caradonia and Grandizia uglier than ever, because during this time the ass's tail on her forehead had grown once more longer than ever.   The King's anger could not be described, though he did not stop to punish the two wicked women then, but ordered his escort to ride back to the wood at once and as fast as possible.   He rode in front, and the kittens ran on before him showing the way.   In the thick of the wood they found the cask; it was hidden under a lot of branches, but the kittens went straight to it, so that the King did not lose time in finding it. When the cask was opened they found poor Cecella, dressed in dirty rags and fainting.

Remembering the kittens' advice, the King gave his bride some fruit to eat, and when she began to get better he took her on his own horse, for he did not risk leaving her alone with Caradonia and Grandizia any more, and off they went galloping to the city.

The King's palace stood high above the town ; it was all made of white marble and pure gold, and as they reached it the building shone dazzlingly in the glorious setting sun.   Round the palace there was the loveliest garden full of rare flowers and tall trees that shaded with their luxuriant foliage the soft green lawns.   To this place the King took his lovely bride, and in these beautiful surroundings, joyful in the love of her husband, Cecella forgot all her misfortunes and lived a happy life for ever after.

As for Caradonia and Grandizia, they were turned into marble statues, and made to support the balcony of Cecella's bedroom.   From that day kittens became great favourites in all the kingdom of Dolabella, and the palace was always full of them.   Both the King and Cecella loved them dearly, for to them was owing their present happiness.

THE
THREE
POMEGRANATES

MANY years before your time, there lived in a wonderful land where the sun always shone and the skies were ever blue a prince whose name was Cenzullo : he was the heir to the throne, and all his subjects were very fond of him because, besides being one of the kindest princes that ever lived, he was also one of the handsomest. In the whole of Terrachiara you could not have found such a tall, strong young man with such lovely jet-black wavy hair and dark eyes so full of light.

In the kingdom of Terrachiara there lived too a cousin of Cenzullo's called Leandro ; he was engaged to be married to the Lady Clarice, who was very ambitious and wicked, and as, should Cenzullo have died, the kingdom of Terrachiara would have fallen to Leandro's lot, Clarice was always trying to persuade her fiancé to find some means of getting rid of poor Cenzullo, so that one day she should be Queen.

In order to carry out this wicked plan, Leandro and Clarice took into their confidence Fata Morgana—a wicked old witch who lived by the sea-shore and fed on seaweeds and crabs. Her one aim in life was to harm other people whenever she could, and more than once she had caused the little fishing-boats that sailed gaily on the deep blue sea to be wrecked upon the crags that surrounded her dwelling.

Morgana was much pleased when Leandro and Clarice called on her, because she loved wicked people, and she took at once a keen interest in their wishes. After they had discussed them for some time, they all agreed that it would be much more effective and less dangerous to cause the poor Cenzullo to die a slow death, and, before the two left, Morgana handed them a syrup that they were to give to the Prince ; this syrup was a mixture of seaweeds, cactus, shell-dust, and the fruit of the poison tree, which they were to pour—a few drops at a time—into the Prince's soup.

Leandro followed Morgana's instructions very carefully, and the consequence was that in a short time poor Cenzullo began to lose his strength and colour ; he could no more go out a-hunting as he used to do, and after a while he was so weak that he was hardly able to lift a spoon to his mouth, and also he could laugh no more.

When the King saw his only son pining away so sadly in his best years, he was exceedingly grieved, and calling to him an old astrologer, he inquired if he could suggest any remedy to bring Cenzullo back to his usual cheerfulness. The old man consulted some ancient books, and finally said that the Prince was under a spell, and the only thing that could break it would be a good laugh.

The next day it was announced throughout all the land of Terrachiara that there was to be a great tournament in the big square, to which all the people of the land were invited, and a reward was promised to the man, woman, or child who should be able to do anything that might cause the Prince to laugh.

On the appointed day Prince Cenzullo was sitting on his balcony with his friends, looking worn and weary and sad, so sad that it made one weep just to look at him. It was lovely weather, the sky was of the deepest blue, the birds were flying about singing and chirruping gaily, and the gardenias and tuberoses perfumed the air with their delightful scent. The square was full of people, and all looked very gay and danced and skipped about : jesters and jokers and conjurers all tried their very best and their funniest turns, but no one was there who could succeed in making the Prince laugh.

Among the crowd, always on the look-out to see whether she could

"ALL LOOKED VERY GAY AND DANCED AND SKIPPED ABOUT."

prevent anything that might have the desired effect, was Fata Morgana, disguised as a wrinkled, shrivelled old woman, looking such a sight that really one could hardly have refrained from laughing just to look at her. And, as luck would have it—or perhaps it was that the good fairies took pity on Cenzullo's unhappiness,—anyhow, as she was pushing her way through the crowd to see better was what happening, she tripped over a huge sack full of flour, and as she lay there, kicking her heels and shouting angrily, as white as a fish that is just going to be fried, she looked such a funny sight that Cenzullo was suddenly seized by a giggling fit, and he went on laughing and laughing while his strength was coming back to him, and he was once more the handsome Prince, the pride and glory of the whole of Terrachiara.

You can imagine the rage of Morgana when she realised that she herself had made her own spell to be broken, thus causing the recovery of the man she wished to be dead ! However, she was powerless to undo what had been done, but she managed to get her revenge by shouting as she passed underneath the balcony : " Prince Cenzullo, pride and glory of Terrachiara, may you never have a moment's peace until you have found the Three Pomegranates and have married one of them," and having spoken thus she waved her wand and disappeared into her grotto.

On the following day Cenzullo set forth in quest of the Three Pomegranates, having first received from his father a pair of iron boots, for the journey was long and difficult. The Pomegranates were kept and carefully guarded in a strong castle built on the top of a mountain by the witch Creonta, two thousand miles away, and great were the difficulties to be overcome, and many a gallant young man was said to have died in the effort to obtain them.

On and on went Cenzullo, all alone, along dusty roads, alpine passes, deep ravines, through marshes, bogs, and swamps, across swift rivers and deep lakes, until he was very tired, and the iron boots were beginning to wear out. Then at last, one fine day, he came in sight of a steep rock on the top of which was a castle built of black stone. It looked very fearsome and inaccessible.

Cenzullo sat down on the grass, and as he gazed at the goal of his ambition, he tried to think how he could possibly ever get to the castle, be admitted inside, and take the Three Pomegranates, without being killed and eaten up by Creonta. As he was thus musing, a tiny dwarf came near him and said in a little shrill voice : " Please pick me that orange ? I am so thirsty, and I cannot reach it by myself."

Immediately Cenzullo got up, reached the orange, which was hanging on a tree next to him, and gave it to the dwarf, who at once began to grow and grow and grow, until he grew so tall that he reached the top of the tree.

" Good Cenzullo," said this strange creature, " you are the first of all the seekers of the Pomegranates who has paid attention to me and done me the little service which I required. You shall be rewarded for your kindness. Come with me and I will tell you how to get to the Pomegranates without being slain."

Thus saying, he led the astonished Cenzullo to a tiny cottage hidden amongst the trees, and when they were inside he gave him some grease, two loaves of bread, and a hand brush, saying : " Listen carefully to what I tell you, Cenzullo. When you reach the top of the hill you will find yourself before huge gates that will close as you come near them. But take this grease and carefully rub the hinges, then you will see that the gates will open

by themselves. As you enter the courtyard a fierce and hideous dog
with two heads will rush upon you to tear you to bits. Do not be
frightened, but throw these two loaves to him, one into each mouth. A
little further on you will find a baker who is sweeping his oven with
his own hands, and he will try to take you and throw you into the
heated oven; but you give him the brush and he will leave you alone.

"Further up you will see a big rope rotting in a dirty puddle; you
take it up carefully and put it in the sun to dry. When you have done
all this, you will find yourself before a marvellous tree, on which, amidst
a bower of wonderful red blossoms, are the Three Pomegranates.
Take them without touching the flowers, which are poisoned; then,
hiding them in your coat, run away as fast as you can. But bear this in
mind : do not open the fruits until you come to a place where there is
drinking-water."

Cenzullo was greatly cheered when he heard all this, and, having
thanked the good giant-dwarf with all his heart, proceeded to climb the
steep hill, and found everything just as his adviser had told him. Wisely,
Cenzullo followed very carefully the directions he had received, and
finally was able to pick and stow away in his big pockets the objects
of his long and tiring quest.

But just as he had finished gathering the Pomegranates a big
magic mirror in Creonta's room fell to the floor and was broken into a
thousand pieces ; and in these pieces the witch saw Cenzullo running
away with her precious fruits, upon which she shouted out in a terrific
voice : " Rope, rope, hang the thief ! "

" Not I," said the rope; " for centuries have I been left miserable
and neglected to rot in that dirty pool. This man has taken me out
and put me in the sunshine : I shall do him no harm."

" Baker, my faithful baker, take the thief and burn him in your
oven ! " next entreated the witch.

" Not I," answered the baker; " for years and years have I toiled
to clean the oven with my own hands. This man has given me a brush.
Let him go in peace."

" Malvagio, my precious dog, slay the thief as you have done to
so many before ! "

"GIVE ME SOMETHING TO DRINK."
From "The Three Pomegranates."

"Not I," growled Malvagio; "for months and months have I been starving to death; this man has fed me. I shall certainly not harm him."

"Gates, my dear old gates, shut yourselves and crush the thief!"

"We shall do no such thing," creaked the gates as they opened to let Cenzullo through. "For centuries we have been eaten up by rust. He has greased us and we feel so happy. We shall let him through without harming him."

At this, Creonta uttered a dreadful shout, and as she did so, a glaring flash of lightning fell on the hill and consumed the wicked witch, the castle, and all that was in it, so that nothing remained, and the spot was left desolate and barren.

Meanwhile Cenzullo was running away with his three Pomegranates, and although he was longing to open them to see what would happen, he remembered well the dwarf's advice, and waited patiently until he came near to a fountain.

Having wended his way once more through mountains, meadows, and forests, he finally reached a beautiful grove where under the shade of a magnificent mimosa tree in full bloom

there babbled and chattered a fountain of the purest crystalline water, which flowed away through the soft green grass in a meandering rivulet.

Cenzullo then sat himself on the grass, amongst which blossomed the prettiest flowers, and having taken out the Three Pomegranates he proceeded to open the first with his knife. Lo and behold! a beautiful girl stepped forth from it, who curtseyed to him and said: " Give me a drink."

The Prince was so astounded at the sight that he took no heed of her demand, but gazed at her in rapture. Then suddenly the lady vanished, leaving no trace whatever.

Cenzullo, greatly disappointed, took up his knife once more and

proceeded to open the second pomegranate ; again a beautiful girl came forth, who curtseyed and said : " Give me something to drink." But Cenzullo had nothing with which to fetch the water, and as he ran about madly trying to find some sort of vessel, the lady vanished out of sight just as the first had done.

Poor Cenzullo nearly tore his hair out in despair, and to avoid further misfortunes he looked round and found a little white shell, which he filled with water and put by him in the shade. Then he began to open the third pomegranate, greatly wondering whether this one would also contain a beautiful girl, or whether it would be empty; and if the lady would run away and leave him more in despair than ever. But as the pomegranate was opened out came a vision of surpassing beauty, her face as white as snow and as pink as the leaf of a rose, her eyes as blue as the sky of Terrachiara, and her hair a mass of flowing gold. Cenzullo was dazzled with the sight, for never in his life had he seen anything so marvellously beautiful; yet he was determined not to lose such a precious gem, and when the lady said: "Give me something to drink," he immediately proceeded to give her the contents of the white shell. The beauty drank it, and then gave her hand to Cenzullo with the perfect manner of a queen, and the Prince was almost beside himself with joy, seeing this splendid reward for all his troubles and dangers.

After Fioralisa had agreed to become Cenzullo's bride, the Prince, wishing her to enter Terrachiara in a manner that was befitting a queen, asked leave to run home and fetch a carriage and horses and attendants and some fine dresses, so that she should enter the place according to her royal position. To this Fioralisa readily consented, and said that meanwhile she would climb the mimosa tree and hide in the branches, for she did not wish to be seen by anybody. Cenzullo helped her up the tree, and then went off hurriedly, for he was eager to show the inhabitants of his country the wonderful beauty of his long-sought bride.

But Morgana, who was furious at having been baffled by Cenzullo and the dwarf, thought out a new plan to harm him and his bride. She quickly despatched her servant Smeraldina, who was the most hideous negress that ever lived on this earth, to kill poor little Fioralisa before Cenzullo came back.

Presently Smeraldina Mora, a pail on her arm, came up to the fountain and saw the image of Fioralisa reflected in the water, and the sight of someone so beautiful made her feel exceedingly jealous, and the more anxious to carry out her wicked mistress's wishes. "Oh, the loveliest of all flowers of the earth!" cried the negress, looking

up through the branches of the tree, " tell me how come you to be hidden in the branches of a mimosa when you should be shining in some beautiful court ? "

Fioralisa, who was as innocent as she was beautiful, told Smeraldina how the Prince had gone to fetch a carriage to drive her to Terrachiara, so that Smeraldina was quite sure that this was the creature she was to kill, and said : " Pretty lady, if you will allow me, I will come up the tree and do your hair in such a way that you shall be a thousand times more beautiful, and Lord Cenzullo will love you even more."

" Oh, I beg you, come up and make me more beautiful!" cried Fioralisa eagerly.

And the malicious creature, climbing up and sitting behind the girl, pretended to be combing her hair, but instead of that she took out a pin and stuck it into Fioralisa's head, and instantly the beautiful girl was changed into a dove and flew away; then Smeraldina threw off her rags and waited in the mimosa in the place of Fioralisa, like a horrid black stone in an emerald setting.

You can imagine Cenzullo's rage and astonishment, when he came back with all his retinue, to find a hideous witch instead of a lovely fairy ! Fain would he have killed her, so great was his wrath; but the crafty slave said : " Do not be angry, my Prince. The sun has thus turned me black while I was waiting, but I shall soon recover my true colour."

There was nothing to be done. Smeraldina was dressed in the magnificent bridal dress that was prepared for Fioralisa, and the cortège moved on towards the town, the Prince crimson with rage at the thought of what his people would think of him, for he had promised them a rare and exquisite beauty, and he was now bringing home an ugly, black-faced negress.

Great was the surprise of the King and Queen when they saw this sight ; yet, as all things were in readiness, the wedding feast began, and there were such festivities as Terrachiara had not seen for many years.

But at the wedding dinner, as Cenzullo was sitting by his horrid bride, looking a picture of misery and disappointment, a white dove flew through the open window into the room and perched on the Prince's shoulder. Smeraldina, when she saw this, tried to catch the bird, but Cenzullo took it into his hand and began to stroke it quietly, and the dove flew once more on to his shoulder and whispered in his ear :

" Beautiful Prince, who art going to be wed,
Take now, I beg thee, the pin from my head."

When he heard this, Cenzullo felt with his fingers the dove's little head, and found the pin and drew it out carefully ; and suddenly there appeared Fioralisa in all her marvellous beauty, just as she was when she had hidden in the mimosa tree.

Almost beside himself with joy at having recovered his true bride, the Prince ordered that she should be dressed in the finest wedding gown that could be found in the palace. He then led the beautiful Fioralisa, lovelier than ever under her flowing veil of lace and silver, to the King and Queen, and told them how the wicked Smeraldina Mora had caused her to be transformed into a dove so that she could take her place. Then, by decree of the King, Smeraldina and Morgana were tied together and thrown into the sea, so that they should do no more harm. As for Cenzullo and Fioralisa, they married and lived happy for ever after in the beautiful land of Terrachiara, and no Princess has there been ever since that could equal in beauty the Princess of the Pomegranate.

LITTLE GOOD-FOR-NOTHING

ONCE upon a time, there lived in a little stone cottage, near a tiny hamlet on the slopes of the Apennines, a woman called Zia Maria, who had a daughter of about seventeen called Rosella. Rosella was one of the prettiest girls of the neighbourhood; many people thought she was quite the prettiest in the country for miles and miles around. Her jet-black hair hung in lovely curls all over her shoulders, her eyes were large and bright, of the colour and brilliance of the beautiful sky above : with her daintily chiselled features, her rose-pink complexion, and tall and slender as she was, she would indeed have passed for a great beauty, but there never trod upon earth such a dreadfully lazy little person. Owing to this, and in spite of all the mother could do, her clothes were always in rags ; her hair, untidy and tangled, hung about her face and neck like a wild growth of some kind ; her face and hands seemed never to have been in water ; and altogether she was quite an unpleasing sight, in spite of her great natural attractions. In the village she was generally known as little " Good-for-Nothing " : never did she do a thing in the house or in the fields to help her mother, but spent her time hanging about, gossiping and sleeping in the shade of a fine chestnut tree that grew in the courtyard of her home.

Over and over again Zia Maria had told Rosella that, unless she changed her lazy ways, she would come to a bad end. The girl was not bad-natured; on the contrary, she was rather a sweet-tempered little thing; but that dreadful laziness of hers prevented her from attending to what she was told and so improving herself.

This kind of thing went on for quite a long time. Finally, one morning Zia Maria lost all patience, and calling out to Rosella, who was still lingering in bed, she said :

" Rosella, I am tired of you. To-day you'll have your last chance. I am going to market now, and expect that when I come back you will have made the cottage tidy, have gathered the vegetables and fruit for supper, and have cooked the meal. If you disappoint me, I'll beat you as you never have been beaten, and throw you out of the house for ever."

When she heard this, Rosella began to cry, and she promised that she would carry out carefully all her mother's orders. So Zia Maria took up the basket with the eggs, butter, and fruit, and marched off to market, after casting one last, threatening glance upon her erring daughter.

When she had gone Rosella looked at all the things she was supposed to do, then she said to herself :

" There isn't really very much. I'll get it all done in no time. I really must do it, as mother was in earnest this morning, but there is plenty of time to do it in. Mother will come in very late. I can do it all in the afternoon, without spoiling the fine morning by stopping indoors."

So she went out, leaving everything in a dreadful state of untidiness, and threw herself on her favourite place in the shade, eating some figs and peaches she had found in the larder. With this pleasant occupation time fled very rapidly. And at last, when with a start Rosella came out of dreamland, the sun was setting in a glory of gold beyond the dark chestnut woods, the evening birds were beginning their songs, and the peasants were coming home from the fields, singing in chorus, their tools on their shoulders.

The girl, somewhat frightened, rose in a hurry, ran to the house, lit the fire, and put the meat on. But she forgot the water, so that when she presently came back from the garden covered with mud, as she had been trying to dig up some potatoes, she found all the meat and nearly all the bottom of the pan burnt, and the room so full of smoke that it nearly choked her. Just at this moment Zia Maria came in, quite tired out with all the work and the walking she had put in during the day, to find a dirty and dishevelled Rosella fussing about a smoky room, where the floor was still covered with dust, the beds unmade, and the supper burnt and done for. Zia Maria's anger was very great; without a single word she seized her daughter and began to beat her mercilessly with a wooden rod.

A few minutes later, as the beating was still going on, the King, who was very young and handsome, happened to pass by. Hearing Rosella's piercing screams, he sent two men from his suite to see what was the matter, as he did not approve of his subjects wailing so loudly without his knowing the reason why.

The officers came in, and as Zia Maria saw them coming up the gravel path she went out to meet them, and, to a question from the men, she replied: " I had to beat my daughter. She has such a

"IF YOUR MOTHER HAS REALLY TOLD THE TRUTH, YOU SHALL BE MY WIFE."

mania for work that while I was out to market she spun all the wool of my mattresses."

The officers went back to the King and reported the answer. The King's astonishment was great when he knew that he had among his subjects such a lover of work, and he said that he would see her. So all the suite came up to the cottage, where in the meantime Zia Maria had been tidying up Rosella, who looked now what she really was, a perfectly charming little thing.

After looking at her, the King said : " I am going to test whether your mother's words were true. You shall now be taken up to the palace. If your mother has really told the truth, you shall be my wife ; otherwise your punishment will be very great indeed."

The King's palace was built on a height, and it dominated the whole valley. It was surrounded by wonderful gardens and parks, that seemed unending, where little rivulets babbled about, and deer and fawns grazed playfully on the fresh grass in the shade of the stately trees. The rooms were all decorated with silver and gold ; hundreds of powdered flunkeys were to be seen everywhere, ready to attend to the King's slightest wishes.

Rosella was taken to a large room in the basement, full of raw cotton and silk in an enormous quantity. In a corner of the room was a spinning-wheel.

" Do you see ? " said the King to Rosella, who was looking about her quite bewildered ; " all these things are for your trousseau ; in a fortnight it must be spun into fine thread and silk. If your mother's words prove true, you shall be my Queen and share with me this lovely palace. But if I have been fooled . . . " Here he made a menacing gesture and went out of the room, leaving Rosella all alone to her work.

Rosella hardly knew how to spin ; to do it all she ought to have worked very fast and perfectly almost all day and night. But the sight of so much work nearly made her sick, and she spent her time eating all the good things that had been left outside the door for her, so that she should not be disturbed, and looking out of a small window at the lovely grounds.

Time went on. Suddenly Rosella became aware that she had only three days left to do her work in, and then she shuddered. It would not be wise to incur the King's wrath. Perhaps they would kill her, or else shut her up in a dark prison and leave her there to pine away and die. . . . The child began to bewail her laziness, and tried to sit down at the spinning-wheel; but she had no practice and she did the work badly. Besides, it was out of the question that even half of it could be completed in so short a time. In despair the girl threw herself on the floor and began to sob her heart out. Presently she heard a small voice saying: " What is the matter with you? and why are you crying so loudly ? "

Rosella looked up and saw peeping down from the window an ugly little creature, all wrinkles and bones, sitting astride on a stick; it was the first thing to speak to she had seen since the day she was brought to the palace, so she told all her troubles.

The old woman listened carefully; then she said in a thin, shrill voice: " I'll get you out of this trouble, but you must promise me one thing."

" What is it ? " cried Rosella. " I'll willingly give you anything that it is in my power to obtain for you, if you will only get me out of this dreadful state."

" Well, you must promise to let me have the first dress the King gives you after you have married him."

This was easy enough, so Rosella promised to do so with glee, and she went and sat in a corner of the room. Meanwhile the old hag hurriedly produced a small golden spinning-wheel that began to revolve so rapidly that one could hardly see it. At midnight on the last day that the King had set for the work to be done, both old woman and spinning-wheel disappeared out of the window, sitting on the same old stick, and to Rosella's astounded and dumbfounded eyes appeared thousands and thousands of skeins of the softest silk and the finest thread beautifully tied together with lovely pale pink ribbons. It was a fine sight indeed, and Rosella began dancing about, clapping her hands with joy.

In the morning a great noise was heard in the passage outside, and presently the King came in with the Dowager Queen, followed by all the ladies and the gentlemen in waiting.

Great was the surprise of everyone when they saw all that work so beautifully done : the King could not believe his own eyes. After they had touched and admired it, the King led Rosella to another room where was a weaver's loom, and he told her that he was quite pleased with the work she had done so far, but now she must weave the lot into fine silken and linen cloth, and get it done in a fortnight. After which he went off once more, leaving the child alone.

Rosella hated weaving and, of course, she was no good at it. Besides, there was too much to do, and also it was the kind of work that only a very skilled and quick worker could have accomplished in so short a lapse of time. Again she spent all her hours eating and sleeping and looking at the skeins, which were so artistically grouped that they formed a charming effect. And time went on—it is a wicked little way of his—and all at once Rosella realised that three days would pass, and then she would incur the King's anger through her laziness and neglect. How silly she was, she thought, not to have tried at least ! Perhaps even if she had done only half the quantity she might have been forgiven for the good work done before. . . . Now all this fine chance had gone for ever. She felt so unhappy that she began to cry, not knowing what to do. As she was sobbing, another little wrinkly creature, possibly the sister of the one who had come before, came through the ceiling and alighted brightly at Rosella's feet without leaving any visible signs of her passage.

" Well, my beauty, and what is the trouble ? " she inquired.

Rosella waved her hand towards all the skeins lying about in rows, and explained how the matter stood.

" Only that ? Well, don't let us spoil those beautiful eyes of yours through unnecessary weeping. Everything will be all right if only you promise to let me have the first dish that shall be served on the table at your wedding dinner."

Rosella dried her tear-dimmed eyes. After all, the request was very reasonable, and she thought that it might not be so difficult for her to get hold of that first plate and have it put aside. So she promised she would

do so : there
was nothing
else to be done,
and the girl
was frightened
to death lest
she should be
thrown into
the palace dun-
geons. The old
woman then
produced a
small golden
loom which
began to jump
about and play
amongst the
skeins. It was
the funniest
sight you ever
saw ! There
was the old
witch, her
pointed bon-
net on one ear,
sitting on the

top of her stick, flourishing frantically her magic wand in all directions,
muttering strange words ; and there was the shuttle rushing about the
room, working as hard as it could. This lasted three days, at the end
of which time the old woman disappeared as she had come, through
the ceiling.

When on the morning of the appointed day the King and his suite
came in to see whether everything had been duly carried out, they were
struck with wonder. On the shelves, all round the walls, were yards
and yards of finest silk and wonderful linen cloth, beautifully woven and

tied with pink and blue ribbons.   Resting against one of the shelves was
Rosella, smiling cheerily and radiantly beautiful, her bright blue eyes
more full of life and light than ever.

The King greatly wondered at Rosella's cleverness and, taking her
little hands in his, said that her trial days were now soon to be over.   All
that cloth was to be sewn into a trousseau in the next fortnight; then he
would take her for his Queen and make her life as happy as possible.

When they had all gone, Rosella, dancing with joy at the thought
that she was really going to be a Queen, began as usual to eat, and it
never entered her head that she might at least have tried to begin the
sewing of her trousseau.

" Some good fairy will come to the rescue," she said to herself;
" why should I worry ? "

As it was, she spent her time as usual, eating, sleeping, and doing
nothing until there were only two and a half days to pass before the
appointed time, and no one had made any appearance as yet.

Rosella was just beginning to get rather dismayed, when, all of a
sudden, a hideous old hag came peeping through the floor.

" Ha, ha ! here we are, my beauty ! I was a little delayed by a
meeting we held last night in the Thick Forest. So you want your
trousseau sewn for you, eh ? "

" Oh yes, good fairy ; please do help me ! "

" Well, I have really come to do that, but you must first promise me
that, unless you guess my name, you will give me your first-born son."

" Oh ! " Rosella staggered back in horror. Should she ever have
a dear little pink-and-white babe sent to her, she should have to give it
to that horrible wretch ! Never !

" I must also warn you," went on the witch, " that unless you
promise to do as I have told you, not only will I not make your trousseau,
but the work done by my sisters will get undone by magic, and the King
shall know how you have deceived and cheated him, and he will have
you hanged for it."

Rosella thought hard for a moment ; then, suddenly making up her
mind, she cried : " Very well, I accept your terms."

The witch, smiling an ugly smile that distorted her hideous features,

took out a golden
needle and set to
work. At the
end of two and
a half days, just
as the clock was
striking twelve,
she disappeared
through the
floor, waving a
wrinkled hand to
Rosella.

"Don't you
forget to bring
me the baby!"

When the

King and his followers arrived in the morning, they all stared in wonder
at the lovely garments so beautifully sewn and arranged on the shelves.
But, as Rosella stood pale and silent, all the light gone from her eyes,
the King went to her and took her tenderly into his arms. "How
pale and worn out you look, my poor darling!" he said; "how can I
have been so cruel as to let you overwork yourself in that wicked way?
From this day you shall do no more work of any kind, for to-morrow I
will marry you, and you shall be my Queen."

On the next day there was indeed a lovely wedding, and Rosella
looked too beautiful for words in her fine bridal dress of silver and gold.
Already the girl had put on one side the first of the many beautiful
dresses given her by the King, saying that it was a vow she had vowed;
and at the wedding dinner the King made no difficulty whatever in
allowing her to have the first dish to be taken up to her apartments, as
he thought it was some fancy of his beloved little wife. And in the
night, as the King was still in council with his ministers, Rosella put on
a big, dark cape, took up the dress and the dish, and ran to the Forest.
Very soon she found the cottage and the three witches sitting in a circle
by the fire.

" That's splendid ! " cried the first two witches, seizing eagerly their things. " Don't you forget *my* lot! " cried the third, as Rosella was running out, trembling with fear lest she should have been seen by anyone, or missed by the King. As it was, nobody had seen her; the King was still with his ministers when she came back, and all had been well.

For some time everything went on beautifully in the palace. Rosella was very happy indeed, for the King loved her dearly and was always ready to grant her all she wished; but there was always that horrible thought lurking in the background of the promise made to the witch that she should have the first baby. And when, after a while, a dear little baby was really sent to Rosella, the King being wild with happiness, the poor little Queen worried so much that she was put to bed with a high fever, and all the doctors of the kingdom were very anxious about her state, as she never seemed to get better at all. The King especially was dreadfully sad and always tried to cheer her up, talking of the dear little child that was growing prettier every day. But Rosella's wonderful eyes were dimmed with tears, and she could not be cheered in any way. Often in the night, when everything was silent in the great palace, the little Queen would get up, go on tip-toe to the cradle where the little darling lay, take it into her arms and cuddle it and hug it, whispering softly : " My own little darling ! You never shall be given to the witch ; I would rather die a thousand times." Yet the days went on, and the Queen knew that it was high time that she should keep her promise ; otherwise the witch would surely take a terrible revenge. This, of course, made her worry even more, and everyone in the Palace was unhappy because the beautiful Queen could not be restored to health.

Now it happened that one morning the King went out with a friend to see whether some order he had given had been carried out, and as they walked in the Thick Forest they passed near a tiny cottage from which came curious sounds.

The two friends then stopped a while to listen, and drawing near they could see through a funny little lattice window three old women, the one uglier than the other, sitting in a circle round a big chimney fire on which an enormous copper was boiling. The oldest and ugliest of the three, the one with a long, pointed nose that seemed to reach her

"THOUSANDS OF SKEINS OF THE SOFTEST SILK."
From "Little Good-for-Nothing."

chin, was blowing the fire to make it flame, and at the same time she sang a kind of sing-song, waving her other hand right and left.

The sight was so strange that the King and his friend stopped a while to enjoy it, and so it was the words of the song reached them. They listened, and this is what they heard :

> " My beautiful Queen Rosella,
>   Thou shalt never know my name.
> My name is Dirindina Dirindella,
>   And it is not known to Fame.

> " When we'll have the little baby,
>   In the copper we shall cook it;
> It will be the daintiest dishlet—
>   With what pleasure shall I hook it ! "

" Oh dear, what a joke ! " cried the King. " Did you hear ? I must really go home and tell my wife. How much amused she will be ! " So they both went back to the palace, and as they went the King kept on repeating the ditty the whole time, lest he should forget it. As soon as they reached home the King ran up to the Queen's rooms. There he found Rosella, very low in spirits, hugging her baby close to her breast.

" Well, my darling, you would never guess what I have seen this morning," cried the King cheerfully. And he told her all about their walk to the Thick Forest, and the witches in the cottage. Then he repeated the ditty, and at the first words Rosella went paler than ever; but as he told her of the witch's name, she suddenly brightened and began to laugh, a thing which she had not done for months.

" Oh dear, how lovely ! " she cried, clapping her hands. " And what did you say her name was, my dear ? "

" I believe it was Dirindina Dirindella—in fact, I am sure of it."

" Dirindina Dirindella ! Oh, how funny ! " laughed Rosella.

" Well, I *am* glad to see you laugh. I was sure the story would amuse you. You look ever so much better." " And I feel better too," said Rosella ; " laughing has done me good."

All that day Rosella kept on repeating to herself the witch's funny name, for fear she should forget it, and at the first opportunity she had of being alone she wrapped herself up in a shawl and ran to the Thick Forest. The three witches were sitting by the fire as usual, and when they saw Rosella come in there came a look of savage joy on their ugly features.

"There, you have come at last!" said Dirindina Dirindella. "You have been long enough. And pray, where is the baby?"

"All right, all right, be patient," replied Rosella. "First I must try and guess your name."

"Oh, my name!" laughed the hag. "Do you really think there is a chance that you may guess it? Nobody knows it, not even the winds. I shall have your baby, and oh! what a lovely breakfast it is going to be for us all!"

"Well, let me try at least," said the Queen. And she began saying all the funny names she had thought of ever since the little baby had been sent to her.

The witch kept on shaking her head, then she growled:

"I told you it was of no use! Come, bring in the baby at once!"

"Shall I really tell you?" laughed Rosella. "Your name is Dirindina Dirindella. Good-bye, and better luck next time!"

And away ran the Queen to the palace, leaving the three witches bewildered and angry.

Needless to say, after this Rosella's health came back entirely, and there was no lovelier sight in the kingdom than she and her little son. You can imagine how proud the King felt! And the three of them lived happy for ever after, Rosella having now learnt that she must be active, and that laziness becomes neither peasant girl nor Queen. The lesson she had received had proved good indeed.

THE HIPPOCRENE LIBRARY
OF WORLD FOLKLORE

Czech, Moravian and Slovak Fairy Tales
Parker Fillmore
> Fifteen different classic, regional folk tales and 23 charming illustrations.
243 pages • 23 b/w illustrations • 5½ x 8 ¼ • 0-7818-0714-X • W · $14.95 hc • (792)

Fairy Gold: A Book of Classic English Fairy Tales
Chosen by Ernest Rhys
Illustrated by Herbert Cole
> Forty-nine imaginative black and white illustrations accompany thirty classic tales.
236 pages • 5 ½ x 8 ½ • 49 b/w illustrations • 0-7818-0700-X • W • $14.95hc • (790)

Folk Tales from Bohemia
Adolf Wenig
> This folk tale collection focuses on humankind's struggle with evil in the world. Delicately ornate red and black text and illustrations set the mood.
98 pages • red and black illustrations • 5½ x 8¼ • 0-7818-0718-2 • W · $14.95hc • (786)

Folk Tales from Chile
Brenda Hughes
> This selection of 15 tales gives a taste of the variety of Chile's rich folklore.
121 pages · 5 ½ x 8 ½ · 15 illustrations · 0-7818-0712-3 · W · $12.50hc · (785)

Folk Tales from Russia
by Donald A. Mackenzie
> Legendary folk tales that weave magical fantasy with the historic events of Russia's past.
192 pages • 8 b/w illustrations • 5 ½ x 8 ¼ • 0-7818-0696-8 • W •$12.50hc • (788)

Folk Tales from Simla
Alice Elizabeth Dracott
> A charming collection of Himalayan folk lore, known for its beauty, wit, and mysticism.
225 pages · 5 ½ x 8 ½ · 8 illustrations · 0-7818-0704-2 · W · $14.95hc · (794)

Glass Mountain: Twenty-Eight Ancient Polish Folk Tales and Fables
W.S. Kuniczak; Illustrated by Pat Bargielski
> As a child in a far-away misty corner of Volhynia, W.S. Kuniczak was carried away to an extraordinary world of magic and illusion by the folk tales of his Polish nurse.
171 pages · 6 x 9 · 8 illustrations · 0-7818-0552-X · W · $16.95hc · (645)

The Little Mermaid and Other Tales
Hans Christian Andersen
> Here is a near replica of the first American edition of 27 classic fairy tales from the masterful Hans Christian Andersen.
508 pages • color, b/w illustrations • 6 x 9 • 0-7818-0720-4 • W • $19.95hc • (791)

Old Polish Legends
Retold by F.C. Anstruther
Wood engravings by J. Sekalski
> This collection of eleven fairy tales "recalls the ancient beautiful times, to laugh and to weep . . ."
66 pages • 7 ¼ x 9 • 11 woodcut engravings • 0-78180521-X • W • $11.95hc • (653)

Pakistani Folk Tales: Toontoony Pie and Other Stories

Ashraf Siddiqui and Marilyn Lerch; Illustrated by Jan Fairservis

These 22 folk tales exude the magic of the Far East.

158 pages · 6 ½ x 8 ½ · 38 illustrations · 0-7818-0703-4 · W · $12.50hc · (784)

Swedish Fairy Tales

Translated by H. L. Braekstad

With 18 different, classic Swedish fairy tales and 21 beautiful black-and-white illustrations, this is an ideal gift for children and adults alike.

190 pages • 21 b/w illustrations • 5½ x 8¼ • 0-7818-0717-4 • W • $12.50hc • (787)

Tales of Languedoc from the South of France

Samuel Jacques Brun

Thirty-three beautiful black-and-white illustrations throughout bring magic, life, and spirit to French folk tales.

248 pages • 33 b/w sketches • 5 ½ x 8 ¼ • 0-7818-0715-8 • W · $14.95hc • (793)

Twenty Scottish Tales and Legends

Edited by Cyril Swinson; Illustrated by Allan Stewart

Enter an extraordinary world of magic harps, angry giants, mysterious spells and gallant Knights.

215 pages • 5 ½ x 8 ½ • 8 b/w illustrations • 0-7818-0701-8 • W • $14.95hc • (789)

Ukrainian Folk Tales

Marie Halun Bloch; Illustrated by J. Hnizdovsky

A unique and merry collection of 12 Ukrainian folk tales.

76 pages • 5 ½ x 8 ½ • 24 illustrations • 0-7818-0744-1 • $12.50 hc • W • (83)

Legends and Folk Tales of Holland

Told by Adèle de Leeuw; Illustrated by Paul Kennedy

Twenty-Eight stories of legendary beasts and familiar animals, of greedy housewives and lovely maidens, of shrewd tradesmen and bold knights, of villains and saints.

157 pages • 5 ½ x 8 ¼ • illustrations throughout • 0-7818-0743-3 • $12.50 hc • W • (120)

Norse Stories

Retold by Hamilton Wright Mabie; Illustrated by George Wright

A rare volume of 17 stories of brave warriors, fierce gods, and exciting adventures.

250 pages • 5 ½ x 8 ¼ • illustrations • 0-7818-0770-0 • $14.95 hc • W • (357)